LEADFOOT

Also by Eric Beetner

Rumrunners

The Lars and Shaine Series
The Devil Doesn't Want Me
When the Devil Comes to Call

A RUMRUNNERS NOVEL

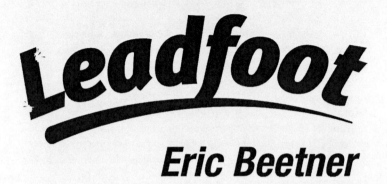

Eric Beetner

**280
STEPS**

1

SOUTHEAST IOWA, 1971

Slow it down, McGraw."

Calvin McGraw, in his natural element—behind the wheel—turned his eyes to the rearview mirror and looked at his passenger through narrowed lids.

"You have any idea who you're talking to?"

The man in back turned away and watched the flat Iowa fields race by out his window.

In the passenger seat beside his father, Webb McGraw grinned to himself. He'd grown up in this seat, hanging on around hairpin turns, getting to know the sound of a V8 as keenly as his own dad's voice. He knew who the man in back was talking to: the best outlaw driver in the Midwest. Maybe anywhere.

Nineteen years old now, Webb had been tagging along on actual jobs with his dad for two years. There were no secrets between McGraw men. Webb knew what his father did. He drove for the Stanleys, a family who would call themselves a criminal empire, but even a nineteen-year-old knew nobody could build an empire in Iowa. An empire of pigs, maybe.

Eyes on the road as he pushed it past seventy, Calvin said to the man in back, "You keeping an eye on the time?"

The man checked his watch. "Ten of."

"Yeah, so if I don't run the cylinders a little hot, we ain't gonna make it. And I never been late yet."

"I know, Calvin. Jeez. I was just sayin'..."

"Well, Bruce, say it to yourself. I know what the hell I'm doing."

What they were doing was a delivery, a big part of the McGraw job. They moved things. Used to be crates of booze. Now it was more drugs, money, people. Anything that needed moving by anything that had an engine in it: Calvin McGraw was your man, and he was grooming his son to uphold the family name. Bringing Webb up in the life came with reservations. Calvin and his wife, Dorothy, had many a late night talk about whether to let Webb find his own way in the world; do something beyond the outlaw life, but so far Webb hadn't shown much interest in anything else.

This was a short run. Eighty-five miles, each way. If Bruce hadn't been so damn late getting to the pickup, they'd be there already. But Calvin didn't need to remind him of that, he only needed to drop his foot a little lower and get them to the meet on time.

Webb acted as navigator and called the turn off.

"Up here, Pop."

Calvin hardly slowed as he spun the wheel on his nearly new Mercury Cougar Eliminator. It took the corner like a champ. In the backseat, Bruce moaned like his stomach was churning. Calvin had heard the sound before.

"You're gonna upchuck, you roll down the goddamn

window. Don't get it on my seats."

They were off the highway on a two lane blacktop road leading into what looked like an ocean of green. Hip high corn stalks rose on either side of the road. A murder of crows took to the air as the Mercury's V8 blasted their picnic with the birdsong of internal combustion.

"There it is," Webb said, pointing to a farmhouse in the distance.

"What's the time?" Calvin asked.

Bruce checked his watch again. "Four minutes 'til."

Calvin slapped the steering wheel. "Hot damn. Streak stays intact."

They parked in a gravel strip near the front of the house. On the opposite side, closer to a worn down barn, was a four door Chrysler sedan. Beyond that lay a rusting tiller at the edge of the corn. Calvin left the engine running. He turned to his son. "You want to drive home?"

Webb's face brightened. "You mean it?"

"Yeah."

The gesture of confidence wasn't lost on the boy. Calvin placed a firm grip on his son's shoulder, his hand still wrapped in a leather driving glove. He squeezed hard and Webb almost winced, but focused on the look of pride in his dad's face instead.

Calvin got out and Webb slid over behind the wheel. Bruce climbed out of the back and waited by the trunk. Calvin removed his spare key and handed it to Bruce who unlocked the trunk. Calvin leaned against the car by the driver's window, unconcerned with what he'd been carrying. Those were the rules—never open the package. Never worry about what's in there. It's not your job. Just get it there and get home safe and don't involve the cops.

Calvin pointed at the wheel. "Hands at ten and two. Never take them off the wheel. Always keep it running. Keep your eyes on your mirrors same as if you were on the highway."

"What for? We're stopped."

"And that makes you twice as easy to ambush. It's a damn sight easier to sneak up on a parked car than a moving one."

Webb had been good at absorbing the lessons. They were getting down to the serious stuff now. Calvin had taught the boy how to drive, a skill he'd been born with in his blood. But the job...in a hundred different ways the job could get you killed faster than a head on collision at a hundred miles per.

Calvin wished his son would cut his damn hair, but he knew that didn't matter. It's what the kids were doing. Cal had never wavered from his high and tight, even if it did show the first stubby grey hairs mixing salt with the pepper. Driving with Webb these days also meant no radio. They just couldn't find a thing there to agree on. Better to let the soundtrack be the rumble of the engine and the rush of wind going by.

Seeing his son behind the wheel gave Calvin a twinge of worry—not something he liked on a job. It's a distraction. And it confused him. Wasn't this Webb's birthright? Could his wife be right? Was it too dangerous? He tamped it down, figured it was just the oddness of being out of the driver's seat. Reminded him of that time he tried to drive one of those little British roadsters with the right hand drive. The mechanics were all the same but damned if it didn't make him feel like he was driving drunk.

"Shouldn't be more than five," Bruce said. "I drop this, then I get the package from him and we're outta here."

"You do what you gotta do. We'll be here."

4

Calvin parked himself by the open trunk, ready to receive the next package. As odd as it was not being behind the wheel, Calvin liked getting the chance to stretch his legs.

It also gave him time to think—a dangerous hobby.

Now north of forty, Calvin had been giving thought to retiring. It was part of Webb's grooming, to make a replacement. But as Webb grew older and the reality appeared on the horizon, he and Dorothy started discussing.

The life of an outlaw wasn't always easy. It wasn't always safe. He had taken gunfire over the years. He'd been in a few close scrapes but—knock on wood— he'd never spent even a single night in jail unless you counted that one night in the drunk tank up in Ottawa. He also knew a streak like that was bound to run out.

His own father had cracked up on a right hand turn he'd taken a thousand times before, and at higher speeds. Something about that day made the good lord call him home, but not without merging his face with a tangle of steel and the sharp metal hands of a speedometer, which, if Calvin thought about it, was about the right way for a McGraw to go.

But he didn't want that for his son, and Dorothy didn't want that for her husband.

The car's idle changed and the brake light by Calvin's knee went dark. He walked back to Webb's window.

"What are you doing?"

"Nothing. I put it in park."

"Did I say to do that?" He didn't wait for an answer. "No. You leave it in gear. Engine on. In gear. Ready to roll." Calvin looked at his son's hands. "And Jesus Christ, ten and two."

Webb lifted his hand from his knee where he'd let it rest. He shrank in the seat, felt his cheeks go hot same as they did when he got scolded as a toddler.

"I'm not saying this just to be saying it, Webb. This is important shit."

"Yes, sir."

He put the car in drive, kept his foot on the brake. Hands in position.

Calvin went back behind the car, drummed his leather-wrapped fingers on the open trunk. The first gunshot came from deep within the house. A second and third came quickly after, each one getting closer.

Calvin tensed, his hands reflexively reaching for a steering wheel that wasn't there. The front door banged open and Bruce came falling out, hands clutching his gut. Calvin jumped to the passenger door, got it open and shoved the front seat forward to make an open path into the back for Bruce.

Another shot splintered against the door frame as Bruce dug a gun out of his coat pocket, turned, and fired a wild shot that banged into the porch wood and burrowed there. The recoil of the gun made it drop from his weakened hand.

"Go, go," Calvin urged him.

Behind the wheel, Webb waited for his father to come take over, his knuckles white in his clock position.

Calvin didn't carry a gun. He never needed one. He waited outside the action, in the car. A disused Browning sat in the glove box, but that seemed miles away now as Bruce stumbled forward like a drunk, leaving a trail of blood down the steps of the porch and across the gravel.

Calvin put a hand on his arm and guided him into the backseat as two men burst through the front door. Cal flipped the seat back into position and slid down into the passenger side. It felt like putting on your pants backward.

"Drive."

A bullet pierced the side of the Mercury and Calvin cringed as if he'd been hit himself. The competition orange color and hood stripes had been extra. To get it repainted would cost a fortune. But Calvin knew they were lucky to get away with their hides.

Webb pressed his foot to the floor and the tires kicked gravel. The trunk lid nodded like it was waving goodbye.

"You know your way out?" Calvin asked.

"Yes, sir."

"Good. Get us to that blacktop and they can't catch us."

This was Webb's test, and he aimed to pass it.

Calvin turned to look behind them but couldn't see past the open trunk lid. He watched through his side mirror and saw what he feared. The two men were getting into the Chrysler.

"You remember what I told you, son. Keep your eyes front. What's ahead of you is always more dangerous than what's behind."

Webb nodded, eyes cemented to the road ahead.

Calvin leaned over the seat to Bruce. He tried not to think about his upholstery when he saw all the blood.

"They got you, huh?"

"Yeah." Bruce kept his eyes and his teeth slammed shut, gritted together to ward off the pain, but it didn't look to be working.

Calvin saw two holes in his gut, and by the looks of what he was leaking out onto the seat, he had another hole in back.

"You hang tight. We'll get you home."

"Those sons a bitches." Bruce lifted a hand to wipe the sweat off his forehead. His hand was so covered in blood he painted his face red. "Fucking Cantrell scumbags."

7

Calvin knew the name of the rival crime syndicate, but he'd never heard of them this far east. Maybe Bruce was talking crazy. Blood loss making his thoughts jumbled up. Or maybe this was a very bad sign of things to come.

Webb turned the Eliminator onto the two lane blacktop and gunned the Boss 429 V8. The narrow hood scoop sucked in air and blew it over the sizzling engine. Webb's hands hadn't moved to any more than 9:55 and 2:03. He stared down the road in front of him like it owed him money.

"Keep her steady," Calvin said. "Looking good, Webb. Real good."

In his mirror, Calvin saw the Chrysler bounce onto the road behind them. They were two football fields away, not a problem for the Mercury to keep that lead. Calvin knew they had guns though. They wouldn't dare fire at this distance... would they?

With his eyes on the mirror he jerked forward as Webb hit the brakes. Tires skidded. Bruce cried out in a harmonizing pitch with the wail of the burning rubber as he flung into the back of the seats.

"Webb, what the fuck are you doing?"

"It was a fox. A little fox or something. Ran right out in front of the car." He was already accelerating again, but he was frazzled. His hands were in the wrong position. He had to downshift to keep the engine from straining.

"So you run the fucking thing over."

"I'm sorry. It was just instinct."

"That's the instinct of a housewife, not a goddamn McGraw. Get your head out of your ass, boy."

The sudden slow down and re-start had slammed the trunk closed and now Calvin had a clear view of the gaining

Chrysler. He could see the man in the passenger seat leaning out the window, pistol in his hand. Calvin looked at his glove box.

It wasn't like he'd never shot a gun. He had plenty of times. Mostly rifles and mostly at deer. This was supposed to be Bruce's job. And Webb was doing Calvin's job. Everything was upside down.

He looked back at Bruce. "How you doing, buddy?"

Bruce had passed out. For the first time in his life, Calvin McGraw was sitting in the shotgun seat.

He opened the glove box, took out the oilcloth inside and unwrapped the pistol. It hadn't been properly maintained and he hoped like hell it wouldn't blow up in his hands if he had to use it. He checked his mirrors one more time. Yeah, he would have to use it.

The first shot from the Chrysler zinged past them. Calvin sucked in a deep breath and pushed it out quick. He pumped the handle on the window and the car was filled with fast moving air and the smell of manure.

"Hold on, Pop. Wait a minute."

Webb swerved the car into the oncoming lane, offering up a better shot for his dad. Calvin leaned out, took aim at the front tire of the chasing Chrysler and let a shot go. The gun fired, but his shot was off. Calvin ducked back inside as two more shots came his way from the Chrysler, which was only twenty yards off their tail now. He knew he didn't look dignified as he cowered and winced at the incoming gunfire. He also didn't give a shit.

"Hang on, Pop," Webb said. "You get ready."

"Ready for what?"

Webb hit the brakes again. The Mercury slowed and the

smell of grinding rubber on asphalt pushed out the manure smell for a moment. With the Chrysler fast approaching, the gap between them closed in a matter of seconds. Calvin found himself side by side with a stunned driver in the sedan.

It took five bullets to get the tire, but he blew the right front wheel on the Chrysler and it spun wildly as Webb stood on the pedal again and shot the Mercury out of there. Calvin watched in the rearview as the blown tire shredded into mulch and the rim of the sedan bit pavement and spun the car, flinging it down into a ditch and ramming the grill into a culvert, flipping the back up over the front until the car landed on its roof amid a row of spring corn.

Webb hollered and slapped the wheel with his right hand. "We got 'em!"

"We did, son. Now get your hands back on that wheel."

Calvin locked the gun back in the glove box and watched his son with pride as the smells of the farmland settled back in over them and the breeze cooled his scalp through his high and tight haircut.

Calvin looked back at Bruce and saw he wasn't breathing. No surprise there. The surprise was what he said about the Cantrells. If it was true, it could only mean bad things ahead. Calvin repeated his own words silently to himself, what's ahead of you is always more dangerous than what's behind.

2

Webb parked the car outside of the Stanley's main office. It seemed a novel idea when they opened shop—criminals having a front office, a secretary, coffee brewing for guests—but the Stanley's prided themselves on appearances. Fine clothes, country club memberships, only the best in front businesses to launder their money and hide their illegal activities from the police and from the other members of the club.

The engine exhaled when Webb turned the key at the end of the hard ride. Webb exhaled too. He could finally relax a little now that they were on friendly territory. It didn't last. Calvin was turned in his seat looking at Bruce in the back.

"Goddammit. Ruined my upholstery."

Webb refused to look. "Why would they shoot him?"

"Same reason any man shoots another—they wanted to see him dead."

Webb felt little comfort in that answer. Calvin dragged a hand down his weary face.

"Guess I'll go break the news."

"I still don't know why we didn't pull over and phone it in."

Calvin looked at his son. "Because news like this you deliver in person, son. And this isn't just about 'ol Bruce here. This is more than just one man dying. Could be we just witnessed the start of something bad. Real bad." Calvin slid out, leaving Webb alone in the car with a corpse. "You stay here."

Webb got out and stood by the front of the car where the smell of hot oil and gasoline fumes overtook the scent of drying blood inside.

Calvin pressed the tiny white button and heard the electronic chimes. The single story office complex had been bought for a song once the previous tenants were convinced it was time for them to move on and move out. The glue outlines of plastic letters left a ghost image of the name Saul Birnbaum, Ophthalmologist, the previous occupant of Hugh Stanley's new office.

The door buzzed and Calvin went in. He passed the outer offices and didn't stop for Cheryl, the busty secretary outside Hugh's suite.

"He's expecting me and he's gonna want to hear this ASAP."

Cheryl waved him in with long red nails like bloody claws. Calvin knocked twice on the door and didn't wait for a response before opening.

"Well, that went to shit right quick."

Hugh Stanley, top man in the organization being the eldest brother of the man who started this mob back during prohibition, sat behind his massive oak desk. Hugh was tall, dark hair oiled back like Dean Martin. He wore a dark blue suit with contrast stitching in white. A deep red shirt, open at the collar and a brightly colored silk cravat where he used to wear a necktie. Calvin liked the old look.

"What did?"

The voice came from Victor Stanley, one of Hugh's younger brothers and the second in command. He sat on a leather sofa facing Hugh's massive desk. His feet were up, a pair of those tall heeled shoes on his feet. He sported a mustache, hair grown over his ears and a silk shirt in gaudy colors, open at the collar and no tie at all. He sniffed, the incessant habit of a cocaine addict.

"Bruce is dead," Calvin said.

Hugh sat up straight in his chair. "He's what?"

"What the hell did you send me into?" Calvin walked to the bar and poured himself two fingers of bourbon on ice.

"They killed him?"

Cal drank half and let the liquor burn down his throat. "Shot him dead and ruined my backseat." He set the rest of the drink down. "Don't you have any beer?"

Victor slammed a palm down on the glass topped coffee table, nearly cracked it. "Those sons of bitches."

"He mentioned the name Cantrell," Calvin said.

"Yes. This did involve them," Hugh said.

"I wasn't aware you did any business with them."

"Not normally, no." Hugh folded his hands across his belly, clear that he wasn't going to offer any further details on the deal.

"Not nearly enough, you mean," Vic said. Hugh shot him a look with all the venom of a cobra. Calvin didn't want to get in the middle of whatever spat they were having.

Calvin waved it away. "It was supposed to be a drop-off, that's it."

"That's all it was."

"Well, it turned into Bruce's funeral." Calvin looked at the unfinished glass of bourbon but didn't pick it up.

Hugh thumbed the intercom on his desk. "Cheryl, get Oscar and two other boys out to Calvin's car right away." He leaned on his elbows and rested his square jaw on his fists. "Good thing we had you out there behind the wheel, McGraw."

"I wasn't behind the wheel, my son was. I was in the shotgun seat and I did not care for it, let me tell you."

"Webb was driving?"

"It was supposed to be a mailman run. Drop off and pick up. I tell you though, the kid did a bang-up job."

Victor sniffed again. Calvin knew the stress of this news made him crave a line of coke, but he didn't dare drop his nose to his brother's glass table and get high. Not around Hugh, the eldest, the responsible one.

Vic fidgeted, bouncing on the couch cushions. "What the fuck are we gonna do, Hugh?"

"We gotta get to the bottom of this."

"I told you something like this would happen."

"Not now, Vic. This thing with Cantrell could be something but I don't want him calling the shots. We don't want to send it off the rails right at the start."

"It looks like he's calling shots already. Now if you'd listened to me and—"

Hugh roared. "Enough, Vic."

Calvin studied the two brothers as he got tired of waiting for a beer and drained his glass, thankful to be above this kind of decision making. He just wanted to drive, not deal with this bullshit.

Hugh tapped his front teeth with his fingernail, thinking. "We just have to think this out."

"Well, for God's sake, don't let Kirby know."

Kirby Stanley came around the corner and saw Webb leaning against the front of the Mercury. Kirby was the younger

14

brother, the oddball. Kirby was quick with a fist, hot tempered and mean. He seemed to enjoy scaring people. He'd taken a near-obsessive interest in the Manson murders a couple of years back and loved to talk about it with anyone who'd let him. Most people in the family avoided him. He didn't even have an office in the building so he was left to hang around the fringes of the business.

Kirby always liked the McGraws. He liked the cars, the speed, the noise.

Webb was as freaked out by Kirby as anyone, but right then he needed what Kirby always had.

"Hey, Kirby, you got a joint?"

"Sure." He reached into the pocket of his fringed vest, the tassels hanging down over his red and orange striped pants. His shaggy hair and worn out hippie threads made him look like someone who'd auditioned, but hadn't made it into The Monkees.

Webb took the offered joint. Kirby held out a zippo and thumbed the wheel. Webb toked and got the joint rolling, relishing the warmth of the smoke hitting his lungs. He wanted to smoke it down to the roach, but he knew it would be rude not to offer a toke to the man who'd just hooked him up, so he held out the joint for Kirby who took it with a pinch of his fingers as he eyeballed the car.

"She looks fast." Kirby took a hit of the pot.

Webb exhaled and rolled his neck, loosening his shoulders. "She sure saved my ass tonight."

"Hit some trouble?" Kirby passed the joint back to Webb.

"You could say that. Made out better than Bruce though." Webb toked and pointed a thumb over his shoulder toward the backseat. Kirby bent over and peered in. When he saw

Bruce sprawled in the back, eyes still open and blood on his shirt—Kirby went black.

He stood up straight as an arrow. "Who did it?"

Webb felt he'd said something he shouldn't have. "I don't know."

"Who killed him?" He asked again.

"He said the name Cantrell. That's all I heard."

Kirby pushed past Webb and nearly took the door to the office off the hinges as he pushed through. *Damn it*, Webb thought. *He kept the joint.*

"We'll set up a meeting," Hugh said.

"Bruce had a meeting with them," Victor said. "How'd that go?"

The door kicked open. Calvin dropped his tumbler. The bourbon was gone, but ice spilled out like dice across the carpet. Kirby came in with heavy footsteps, the smoldering joint still pinched in his fingers.

On the sofa, Victor recovered from the shock. "Jesus Christ, Kirby. What the hell?"

"Cantrell did this?"

Hugh shook his head in frustration. "Calm down, Kirby. We're handling it."

"I'll fucking kill him." He flung the joint to the carpet.

"No, you won't." Hugh stood, holding his palms out like he was talking a bear away from his picnic. "We've got this under control. Okay?"

Kirby stood clenching and unclenching his fists, like two pumping hearts at the end of his arms. He breathed heavily through his nose.

"We got it," Hugh said in a quieter voice. "It's fine. If we need you, we'll call you."

Kirby ran his black eyes over his brother. "That's what you always say." He spun and stomped out, leaving the door open and deep indents from his feet in the shag. The room stayed silent after he left.

Calvin finally broke the spell. "Well, I should get outta here."

"Me too," Victor said and he stood with a long snort. Calvin would head back to the car, see if the men had gotten Bruce's body out yet. Victor would go to his office, pull out his Peruvian hand-carved snuff box and dig out a spoonful. Hugh would stay behind and try to figure this shit out.

3

Calvin crossed the lobby, grateful to be leaving the mess behind with Hugh. Ahead of him, Victor slipped into his office and the door quickly shut. Everyone steeled themselves for battle in their own way, he supposed.

He passed through the front doors and saw three men at work on his car. Bruce was long gone and the backseat would be shortly. The men tugged at bolts, pulled hard at the braces holding the seat in place. Calvin was disgusted. He thought these were the type of men who ripped a woman's dress on a first date, tore open a neckline and said stuff like, "Show me them titties." No grace. No caress. But he was too tired to correct them and show them the proper way to treat a vehicle.

Instead, Calvin stepped off to the side of the building into a small courtyard with a fountain – a leftover from the days of this squat building being a medical plaza. Some place for people to sit out a bad diagnosis, though in this place nothing more serious than the need for bifocals or an impacted molar was ever the bad news of the day.

Times like these, other men would have a smoke. Not Calvin. He'd picked up the habit for a few short years in the early 50s, but it didn't stick. One time he was waiting for a pickup and sat behind the wheel smoking an unfiltered Lucky Strike. When the man sprinted to his door, tore it open and said, "Go, go, go." Calvin needed a moment to toss the smoke. He pitched it, bouncing it off the glass of his window and back into his lap. He choked on the lungful of smoke and had to beat out the orange ash from his crotch. It cost him seconds. Precious seconds. They got out and everything was fine, but he didn't like the feeling. No more smoking on the job. No way.

Calvin thought he might find Webb in the courtyard, but he found another familiar voice.

"Well, well, if it isn't the man with the lead foot."

Nancy Stanley, Victor's wife. She sat on a small bench overlooking the fountain, long dark European cigarette in her hand. Her raven hair was done up in a Jackie Kennedy style she'd adopted the day after the inauguration and hadn't abandoned since. Her lips were deep red, as usual, and her heavily outlined eyes smoldered at Calvin.

This was the way with Nancy. She'd been trying to get Cal in bed for more than a year.

She did a French inhale and thought it looked sexy, like a girl from a black and white movie. Calvin thought it looked like she was trying to give herself smoke inhalation.

"Nancy," he said. Curt, professional.

"You here to give me a ride?"

She tried—and succeeded—in making her every word a sexual entendre.

"Just wrapping up. Letting the boys do a little work on the car."

"So you have time to do a little work on me?"

"Nancy..." Calvin sighed, tired of this game. Not only was

she Victor's wife, but Calvin loved his own wife. Way more than a roll in the hay with an admittedly attractive woman.

"When are you going to lighten up, McGraw? Give a girl a chance."

"Why don't you give your husband a chance?"

"What Victor's been giving me since the night we were married isn't worth taking a chance on. He doesn't know how to treat a woman. Especially when he's got that nose candy running the show below the belt." She pointed to her nose. "Up it goes." Then down to her crotch. "And down *it* goes."

"That's really none of my business, Nancy."

"I'm just saying, you'd be helping a girl out."

Calvin had no doubt there were plenty of younger studs on the payroll willing to help her out, and he was sure they did exactly that. He could see it in her eyes, beyond the makeup— she wanted him because he said no.

"Look, it's been a long night. Things are getting kinda heated in there."

"We could make things downright hot here."

She blew a plume of smoke. Calvin exhaled a tired breath of his own. "Have a good night, Nancy." He turned and walked back toward his car.

"I'll get you someday, Leadfoot."

Calvin ignored her. When he got back to his car he couldn't ignore it any more.

"Boys, boys. Go easy on her, all right? This isn't your high school prom under the bleachers. You gotta sweet talk her a little bit." And he moved in to help.

Calvin and Webb got home well past midnight. Dorothy, Calvin's wife, waited up.

The difference between Dorothy and most wives waiting up after twelve o'clock, was that she was there with hot coffee, a plate of brownies and a smile. She knew everything Calvin did, and had done. They bore no secrets. She knew she married an outlaw and she wore the McGraw name proudly.

"Long one, huh?" she said as they came in the door.

"Too long," Webb said and he excused himself off to his apartment over the garage. At least this late at night they would probably avoid the ear crushing music coming from his stereo and his gnarled attempts to play the guitar like Jimi Hendrix.

Cal sat down at the kitchen counter, let out a long sigh.

"Rough day?"

"Someone got killed, Dot. Died right in my backseat."

"Oh, Cal." She put a hand over his.

"Wasn't anyone I knew real well, but my upholstery is a total loss."

"You really think that's what you should be worrying about right now?"

"It's all I can worry about. There might well be bigger things brewing, but it's my job to stay out of it and I'm happy as a clam to do it."

She patted his hand twice, turned to serve him a brownie off the tray. "I've never seen a clam I could say was any happier than any other creature. And I'd bet there hasn't been a truly happy clam who ever found himself in the state of Iowa."

"You may be right about that."

Calvin kissed her on the cheek, begged off the coffee which she set back on the counter for morning.

"How many more late nights and dead friends is it gonna be before we talk serious about you stepping out?"

Calvin didn't have the energy for this conversation so late

after a hard day, but he figured that's exactly what Dorothy counted on. Get him while his defenses were down.

"It might not be a good time to bail on them right now."

"Is it ever going to be a good time?"

"I s'pose not." He went to the fridge and took out a can of beer.

"The man from Empire Racing said he'd give you until end of summer, right?"

Cal swallowed a mouthful of beer, fighting the foam from overflowing in his over-eager mouth. "That's what he said."

"It's coming up."

Calvin had gotten a job offer from a stock car racing company. His name got around in the world of gear heads, motor maniacs, gas huffers, tire burners, oil jockeys and pit crews. They wanted him to run the team. Train new drivers, teach the old ones some new tricks. They didn't offer to have him drive, though. Too old. That didn't sit well with Calvin.

On the other hand, nobody would be shooting at him on a race track.

"It's not like it's big time or nothing. I won't be crew chief for Richard Petty or nothing."

"Steady work, though. You get to be around cars all day long."

"Yeah, around 'em. Not in 'em."

"Still." Dorothy could remain calm in any situation. She refused to argue with Calvin. She knew he needed to come to a big decision like this on his own. She also knew she was tired of men shooting at her husband. And she for damn sure didn't like the idea of them shooting at her son.

"It means traveling a lot. And not to fun places like Daytona. This is Midwest Regional. State fairs, dirt tracks, small towns."

"I just want to know you're thinking about it, Cal."

"Oh, I'm thinking. When those bullets were coming at us, I was thinking all right. Don't you worry about that."

She set a hand on his. "I never worry, Cal."

"Mrs. McGraw, I work with liars on a daily basis, and you, my dear, are the best damn liar I ever met." Calvin kissed her. "Let's get some sleep."

4

The next day went by with boring familiarity. Calvin slept in until he was woken by Webb's attempts at mastering the guitar part from "Revolution." As he lay in bed scratching at the stubble on his chin he thanked the lord his son was a damn good driver because his guitar playing sounded about as good as starting a car while a possum slept on the engine block.

Dorothy made breakfast, he refilled the bird feeder, they worked on a puzzle of the Statue of Liberty. Life was good. It sure beat working for a living.

Webb went out to be with friends and Calvin and Dorothy found themselves alone in the house. He gave her a look, she lifted one eyebrow back at him and soon they were upstairs making love.

Laying the tangled sheets, one arm around his wife while sweat cooled their skin, he made his decision.

"I think I'm gonna call that fella from Empire Racing."

"Well, don't keep a girl in suspense. What are you gonna tell him?"

"That I'll meet with him. I need to know more before I jump."

"Of course." She leaned over a kissed his cheek. Calvin felt like she was buzzing below the surface. "That's wonderful, Cal. Maybe Webb can work under you?"

"If I'm in charge then I do the hiring I suspect. *If* I take the job."

"How would the Stanleys take it?"

"They're not gonna like it," he said, sliding one hand under his head to catch more of the afternoon breeze coming in the open window. "But it sounds like you're asking if they're gonna have me killed or something. I don't think so."

"You don't *think* so?"

"You never can tell how far they take loyalty. I'm pretty damn sure I've earned my retirement."

"Then let me shut up before I talk you out of it."

Dorothy rolled over and kissed him on the lips. Twenty-two years together and her lips on his still sent a spark down his spine.

The next morning Calvin pulled into a dirt lot outside a race oval. He'd taken the Chevelle SS 454 from the garage that morning and the engine grumbled low. The air was dusty from cars spinning laps around the track. High pitched engines buzzed like overgrown cicadas. A series of squat outbuildings surrounded the track and a small collection of garages lined one side.

A short man in a bright blue shirt with a wide tie that stopped in the middle of his round belly marched a straight line across the lot toward Calvin.

"Mr. McGraw," the man said, thrusting out a hand to meet him. "Marshall Pruitt, Empire Racing. Good to finally meet you in the flesh."

"Nice to meet you, Mr. Pruitt."

"Call me Marshall." He pumped Calvin's hand vigorously

and for longer than Calvin thought necessary. "Come on over to the pits. I figure that'd be a better place to meet than some stuffy old office for a man like yourself. Someone with gasoline in his veins."

Still gripping his hand, Marshall steered Calvin toward the row of garages.

He got the full tour, met the crew, saw the cars, learned about the layout. All throughout Calvin said only a few words. Despite being surrounded by cars and the smell of burning oil, he never felt quite comfortable.

"So," Marshall said after he'd gone on so long Calvin thought there were no more words in the English language to use. "I suspect you have a few questions for me."

Calvin scratched his head. "First off, how did you hear about me? Who gave you my name?" Marshall had been vague about it in their first phone call.

"Word gets around. Good drivers keep their ears to the ground to know who the up and comers are."

"I'm hardly an up and comer, Marshall. I'm forty-two."

Marshall dropped his voice to a whisper. "An old co-worker of yours clued us in." He grinned like he was in on a special joke.

"And why do you think I can train your drivers better than the man you've got now?"

"We've got no man now. Last guy left us for an outfit in Wisconsin. He was for shit anyway, pardon my saying. Kept telling my boys nobody ever finished a race from the back of an ambulance. But you see, Mr. McGraw—Calvin—the folks who come to our races want a little danger. They want to see the kind of driving you're known for. What you've been doing for years. I need you to put a little of the outlaw into my boys."

The word struck him. Outlaw. It's what he was, even Marshall Pruitt knew so. And so did Calvin. It's why he didn't feel like he was among his people at a race track, even though all indications said he should. His people were the outlaws. The stark truth of it nearly knocked him on his ass.

"I'll have to let you know, Mr. Pruitt."

"Of course, of course. You think about it." He set a hand on Calvin's shoulder, had to reach up to do it. "But look at those boys, McGraw." They watched as a trio of young men spun an endless left turn around the track. Calvin agreed, there was no style there. No excitement. Just three cars driving in a loop. It made him think about death and the never-ending march of time. Christ, it depressed him to look at. Calvin turned away.

"They need you, McGraw." Marshall sounded like his boys needed salvation, not driving lessons.

"That's all they ever do is turn left, huh?"

"Well, the track is a circle so..."

One of the boys spun out and his car skidded onto the infield grass and came to a gentle rest.

"I'll be in touch," Calvin said.

In his car he aimed out of the dirt lot. He saw Marshall waving goodbye in the rearview, the wind whipping his fat tie up into his face. Calvin stopped. He revved the engine on the Chevelle and cut the wheel. He picked up speed as he drove past Marshall, kicking dust over the tiny man, and made his way onto the track. He merged onto the oval with the three drivers, the third boy having rejoined the pack.

Despite their race tuned cars, Calvin met them at full speed. He saw grins on the boys and gloved hands tighten on wheels as they welcomed the newcomer to the track. They intended to show the old timer what their stock cars could do.

Calvin tried something he knew would throw them. He turned right. The Chevelle zagged up toward the wall on the high part of the track before zigging back down toward the flats. The three stock cars didn't know what to do. All three braked and Calvin shot ahead.

Behind him he heard the trio of engines pick up speed, the low growl of the Chevelle a full octave beneath the piston whine of the stock cars. He saw them come up by his rear panel, two to his right, one below on his left. Again he swerved, again they backed off, this time in a squeal of tires and fishtailing.

Calvin kept them from passing him for three full laps before he veered off and pulled to a stop beside Marshall who'd been watching with a grin as wide as his tie and his hands clapping themselves to numbness.

"Brilliant," he said. "Exactly what we need."

"Let me ask you," Calvin said. "I don't gotta wear a tie, do I?"

"You can wear a goddamn dress for all I care."

"I'll call you." And Calvin was gone in a whirlwind of dust.

"How'd it go?" Dorothy asked.

"It...went."

"I don't think I want to know, do I?"

"It's a big change, Dot. A lot to take in."

She pulled him into a hug. "I know it is. Thank you for at least trying it out."

"I told him I'd let him know."

"Well, when you know, let me know."

"I will." They kissed and went into the kitchen for a beer.

The next day went as quiet and calm as the day before until about half past four when Calvin got a call from Hugh.

"I need to see you. Something urgent came up."

"Need to be tonight? We were thinking about going over to Farnham's for some ice cream and then to the park."

"It needs to be tonight. Right now. And make sure your car is gassed up."

"Always is," Calvin said. "I guess the dang skeeters would be out in the park anyways."

He hung up and offered an apology to his wife.

"This about that mess from the other day?" she asked.

"I suspect it is. I knew it meant bad news a-coming." Calvin lifted a pair of keys off the row of nails by the door. "Tell Webb I got this one and to hang tight, okay? If this is part of that mess with Cantrell, I don't want him to get tangled up in it just yet."

"Are you gonna say anything to them? You know..."

"I'll have to feel it out. Might not be a good time."

She had something more to say but she held it in.

He kissed Dorothy goodbye and left the Mercury and its no backseats in the driveway. He went into the garage and got out his '68 Dodge Demon. The twin hood vents always reminded Calvin of squinty eyes. He considered it his mean car. It rumbled out of the garage with a low tone sweeter than anything Webb ever hoped to strangle out of his guitar.

Twenty minutes later he parked in front of Hugh's office.

"Got a job for you, Cal."

Hugh didn't bother with formalities or small talk.

"Busy week."

"This one is sensitive. Just between you and me, okay?"

"You think I made it this far by spilling secrets?"

It was a way of reassuring Hugh and also reminding him that, of everyone on the payroll, Calvin probably knew more about where the bones were buried and who they belonged to than anyone else outside of Stanley blood. And it went back to Hugh's own father. Calvin did a few 'just between us' jobs for him and he'd kept a tight lip about them, even from Hugh.

"I need you to go pick up a bit of cargo for me, down outside of St. Louis."

"St. Louis? Shit, that'll take me the better part of two days."

"I need you to leave right away."

Calvin knew better than to argue. This was his job. His lot in life.

"You got an address?"

"Right here." Hugh held up a sealed envelope, but held it back. "But Cal...the cargo is, well, it's a person."

"I didn't ask." He never did. Part of the rules. Don't ask about the package. Not your business, only to deliver it.

"I know, but I didn't want you to be confused when you get there. It's a girl, you see..."

Calvin did see. Hugh didn't need to explain. She'd be blonde, young, stacked up top. Hugh had a dozen of them stashed around. But what was one doing down in St. Louis? And why was it so urgent to get her back up to Iowa? Questions that would have to go unanswered. Just deliver the package.

"You want her back here or to the house?"

"The house." Hugh held out the envelope.

Calvin took it. "I thought this was gonna be more bullcrap with Cantrell."

"Nah. If those Omaha pussies want trouble they're gonna have to work harder than that. I don't need a war right now."

"When do you ever need a war?"

"Christ sake's Calvin, you sound like those goddamn hippies marching on D.C. When did you go in for flower power?"

"I'm just saying is all."

"Yeah, you're just—"

The phone on his desk rang. Calvin used the letter to salute a farewell and headed out while Hugh attended to his new business.

Cal said goodnight to Cheryl at the desk and asked if he could use the phone extension in Victor's office. It being after five o'clock, he knew Vic would be long gone. He'd be nose deep in powder so thick you could ski in it by now.

"Sure, Mr. McGraw. G'head." Cheryl was definitely Hugh's type, but Calvin doubted he'd ever slept with her. He liked to keep his business and his pleasure separate.

As Calvin was hanging up with Dorothy after breaking the news to her that he wouldn't be back tonight, he heard Hugh bellow from his office.

"Is McGraw gone yet?"

"I'm not sure, sir," Cheryl answered.

"Well, shit, see if you can catch him, goddamnit."

Cheryl's high heels tapped on the floor as she came out from behind her desk to chase down Calvin, but he stood and met her at the door to Victor's office.

"Woah, woah there, honey. I'm still here."

"Oh, thank goodness, Mr. McGraw. Mr. Stanley wants to see you."

"Yeah, I heard. Thanks."

Calvin went back into Hugh's office. Behind his massive desk, Hugh looked like he'd been gut punched.

"Cal, thank fucking Christ you're still here. We got a

situation."

Calvin held up the letter. "You just handed me a situation, I thought."

He seemed to have forgotten the girl down south. Hugh slapped his desktop and said, "Shit." He chewed on a knuckle, weighing a choice in his mind. "This is the bigger fish right now."

"Whatever you say." Calvin stuffed the sealed letter in his back pocket and stood still to listen to the new crisis.

"Goddamn Kirby," Hugh said. He rolled the name across his tongue like it was sour. "Kirby went and got himself in a mess."

With Kirby, that could mean a lot of things. "Yeah?" Calvin said.

"He got a bug up his ass about that Cantrell shit that went down and it seems he decided to take matters into his own hands."

"Guess I should have left more directly. I could be on the road to St. Louis right now."

"I need you to go get Kirby."

"Get Kirby? Where the hell is he?"

"In some house full of Cantrell's boys." Hugh sat back in his chair, limp as a scarecrow. "Dead Cantrell boys."

Calvin let out a whistle. Hugh nodded in agreement.

"Guess he went and got a ride with a few of the other guys. Got one killed and the other one tried to run but crashed into a tree and burned up."

"What the hell?"

"Goddamn trouble and grief follow that boy around. And what don't follow him he stirs up and makes for himself."

"Seems like a bit of an escalation, huh?"

"It's an act of fucking war is what it is."

Calvin reminded Hugh of his own words. "And we don't need a war right now."

"Looks like we got one anyhow."

"Does he know I'm coming? I don't want to pull up some place and have him think I'm on the other side of this thing."

"He knows. I told him to sit quiet until you get there. He said it was quiet as a tomb. A fucking joke, I suppose."

"What about the other thing? It can wait?"

"It'll have to, won't it?"

Calvin saw on Hugh's face that he didn't want it to. He tried to ask around the edges without violating the rules.

"It'd be better if it didn't though."

Hugh nodded.

"Because it might turn into a longer trip than St. Louis." State what he thought he knew. Don't ask questions.

Hugh nodded again.

"Send Webb," Calvin said.

Hugh raised an eyebrow. "Is he ready?"

"He got us out of there in one piece yesterday. A straight pickup? He's ready. And he can zip his lip like a McGraw."

Hugh chewed a knuckle while he weighed the decision. "All right. Send him. You get out to Kirby and get his ass back here. I need to have a talk with that boy."

Calvin nodded once and left to give the envelope to his son.

33

5

Seriously?" Webb stared at the sealed envelope in his dad's outstretched hand.

"Yep. It's your time, son."

Webb smiled, took the envelope and thrilled at the formality of tearing it open to reveal his destination. It was like he won a prize. Wouldn't all those assholes at 4H eat their hearts out with their prize pigs and dumbass cows if they could see him now.

"I don't have to tell you the responsibility that comes with this, do I?"

Webb met his father's level stare. "No, sir."

"Well, I'm going to anyway because it's my ass on the line too if you screw this up. You carry something into this job, boy. The McGraw name. That ain't nothing to sneeze at. Me and your granddaddy worked our asses off behind a wheel to earn what that name means nowadays. There are folks pay a lot of money for nothing much more than the badge on the hood of a car because they know it means something. Means quality. History. That's what a McGraw man is. He brings that heritage with him on a job every time he puts his foot down on the gas. That's what you've got in you now, Webb."

Webb nearly blushed with pride until Calvin put a firm hand on his shoulder, squeezed it hard and said, "Don't fuck it up."

Webb nodded and read the paper. An address in a town outside of St. Louis and the name of a girl—Joni. The only instructions were: Get her back here.

The Mercury grumbled louder than normal now that half the insides were a cavern of exposed sheet metal where the backseat used to be. It was lighter so he'd get better pickup, that was a plus. Webb tossed a small duffle bag with a change of clothes in the back and it sank to the floor. He set up a half dozen cassette tapes he'd brought for the ride—The Rolling Stones, Hendrix, Led Zeppelin 3, Derek and The Dominos, The Who - Live at Leeds and T. Rex. With Calvin out of the way he could crank the stereo and enjoy the open road.

Calvin watched his son pull out of the driveway. He hadn't told him of his own assignment. The boy didn't need anything clouding his head on his first solo run. As Calvin watched the Mercury fade away he thought of all the things he didn't tell his boy, like don't fuck the girl. Women in the shotgun seat always came with a side of trouble. He also should have given him a lesson in how to talk—or not to say a goddamn word— to the men he was picking up the package from. Show up, drive the car, get the cargo and go. But shit, this was all stuff Calvin had been educating the boy in since the day he took to two wheels on a bicycle in the park.

Calvin watched with pride. His boy was a man today. He was a McGraw.

A hundred miles west was a house run by the Cantrell clan.

At least it used to be. Calvin didn't have any expectations of what it might look like after Kirby went there with revenge on his mind. He didn't give much thought to what happens to a man when he falls into the tiger cage at the zoo, either. Both were gonna be bloody and both were probably their own damn fault.

The sun had gone down ahead of him as he drove and the stars came out on a moonless night. The highway was Iowa straight, traffic around him light. He looked out over fields on either side of him and watched fireflies blink in the darkness trying to find each other. Grain towers stood lit from underneath, Iowa's version of those redwood trees out on the coast.

Calvin drove with no radio. Cylinders under the hood provided all the soundtrack he needed. The smooth roll of the Demon's tires over ruler-straight pavement made you think the world really was flat. On the job, the only world he needed to know was what could be lit up by a pair of headlamps and seen out ahead of him at eighty miles per on a dark country road.

Right when his internal clock told him he ought to be getting close, he spotted the farm house and slowed the Demon.

Calvin rolled in and killed the lights, watching the house like a wolf stalking prey. It seemed like every light in the house was on, including the barn. Three cars were parked at angles in front. The barn doors were slightly open, swinging gently in the night breezes. He cut the engine and heard nothing outside but the hum of crickets and cicadas.

Calvin waited, but Kirby did not appear. He thought about honking, but something told him not to disturb the deep quiet. Calvin got out of the car.

On the porch he saw the first body. A man, face down, his body looking like he got caught mid stride on his way out the door. One arm hung down from the top step, blood dripping off the fingers and collecting one step below. The front door was open.

Calvin questioned his choice to not carry a gun.

The cicadas quieted and he heard a low hiss. He followed the sound out across the lawn and saw the tail end of a car, the front end smashed into a tree as Hugh described it. Calvin examined the wreck and saw the man behind the wheel, his face dented in the middle where the steering wheel had caved in his nose. A wisp of smoke rose from the engine like a cobra under a spell until it melted away into the night air.

Calvin turned back to the house. He went to the three cars, pressed a flat palm to the hoods. Cold, cold, warm. Not good.

But his cargo was still here and not in his car on the way back to the Stanleys. His job was not over.

Calvin McGraw had spent his fair share of time in harms way at the behest of the Stanley clan. They paid him handsomely for it, but he never got used to it. And he never shied away.

He put a foot on the bottom porch step and listened to it creak—a farm doorbell. A fly buzzed his ear on the way to the stagnant blood pooling around the dead man. As Calvin took the next step he could see in through the open door and to the carnage inside.

Three more bodies were scattered there like throw rugs meant to accent the furniture. He noticed the impossible angle of one man's neck, spun around to look at his own backside. He saw one man face up with his shirt torn open, his chest cut open just as wide. The flies had found him too.

One thing he noticed about all the bodies—they were each missing an ear. He turned to check the man on the porch and sure enough, one ear short. Kirby collecting trophies.

The scrape of a chair from the kitchen. Calvin went there slowly, reluctantly.

Kirby sat in a chair. Metal legs on linoleum tiles. He didn't rise to greet Calvin because he was tied there. Calvin froze as he noticed the two guns pointed in his direction.

"Who the fuck is this?" The man directly behind Kirby spoke in a flat Nebraska accent indiscernible to anyone outside of the two neighboring states.

"This is my ride," Kirby said. "Like I told you."

"You alone?"

The man's hand shook and the barrel of the gun waved in tiny back and forth motions like a nervous insect. Calvin nodded.

"I wanted to talk to a Stanley. Bring me Hugh or Victor."

Calvin looked to Kirby who remained calm, somehow. Calvin waited it out until Kirby spoke.

"They're not coming, dipshit. Like I told you. They don't do grunt work."

Calvin swallowed the insult to his profession and watched the action closely, checking the exits, looking for escape routes.

"But you're their brother." The Cantrell man was more insulted than Kirby that they sent an errand boy to get him.

"Younger brother. You got older brothers? Youngest is the worst. Worse than a middle child. What I wouldn't give to be a Peter Brady. Instead I'm a Bobby."

Kirby smiled. The two gunmen grew more agitated. Calvin stayed still.

"Take me to him." He thrust the gun toward Calvin, the tip trembling in the electric air between them.

"To who?"

"Either one. Someone is gonna answer for this shit."

"This is the answer," Kirby said, anger in his voice now. "Did you forget what you did to our man?"

"That was one guy. This is..." He didn't have the words for the slaughter that had taken place there. Calvin couldn't help him with that, either.

"Payback?" Kirby smiled again, showing blood in his teeth. He turned to Calvin. "Sorry about this, Cal. I thought I was all done here. All I had left to do was gather up some keepsakes." He winked at Calvin who thought of the ears. "I was so busy in my work I guess I didn't hear these assholes pull up.

Footsteps. They all turned. A third gunman came down the stairs. From his position in the doorway to the kitchen Calvin could see him. He looked shell shocked. He had to step over a body on the steps, one Calvin hadn't noticed before. The gunman spread his legs wide to straddle the man, but didn't make it far enough and stubbed the point of his shoe on the dead man's shoulder, causing an avalanche of corpse and live body. As the dead man slid down on a trail of his own leaked blood, he took out the live man's feet and it ended up as a toboggan ride down the steps. When they hit the landing the corpse stopped abruptly against a row of spindles and a handrail while the gunman tumbled off and somersaulted through a puddle of blood and what looked like a severed foot.

"Mother—" the man stood up, slapping his body to get rid of the viscera and the memory. "Fuck!"

"Conrad, calm down," the leader in the kitchen said.

"Yeah, Conrad," Kirby said. "Chill out. Why don't you take a hit of the shit you guys have been growing here."

For that Kirby got a smack on the head from the butt of the leader's gun. He took it in stride.

Conrad continued to freak out. "Is it on me? Jesus, Harrison, do I have blood on me?"

"Relax."

Conrad noticed Calvin for the first time. He stopped his flailing and lifted his gun.

"Here's what's gonna happen," Harrison said. "Wiley's gonna stay with this guy." He used the point of his gun to indicate Kirby and the other, silent, gunman in the kitchen. "Me and Conrad are gonna take a ride with this guy." He pointed the gun at Calvin. "And go see Hugh. Get him to answer for this shit."

The plan had been set, but nobody moved. Calvin broke his silence. "You want me to deliver you right to Hugh Stanley himself?"

"Yeah. You got a problem with that?"

Calvin shook his head.

"No phone calls," Harrison went on. "No warnings. Just like how this asshole shows up here, we show up there. Hand delivered by his own chauffeur."

The muscles in Calvin's arms tensed. His hands clenched into fists. Harrison had used the C word. McGraws did a lot of things for the Stanleys. They were not fucking chauffeurs. Calvin felt like he could do some Kirby style slaughter right then.

"Move, jackass." Harrison pointed Calvin toward the door.

"See you in a bit, Cal," Kirby said. "We'll laugh about this later."

"Shut up," Harrison said. "We got a fucking Stanley brother on the line. Hooked and pulled into the boat, asshole. You're a valuable commodity. You're what we call a bargaining chip."

"What I am is the biggest fucking mistake in your very short life, motherfucker." Kirby let his eyes go dark, showing the side of him that tore through the house earlier. Harrison turned his back on the kitchen and hustled Calvin out the door.

6

Calvin aimed the Demon back across the arrow-straight road headed back east. With each drop of his foot on the gas the engine would growl, like the warning sound of a beast on the hunt. Harrison, in the passenger seat, ignored the noise. Conrad, in the back, filled the car with the humidity and smell of his sweat.

"You guys got a plan?" Calvin asked—eyes forward, hands at ten and two.

"Shut up and drive," Harrison said. The gun rested in his hand, aimed at Calvin's stomach.

"Without a plan it might be real difficult to get what you want." Calvin revved the engine. The beast growled again.

He got no response so he went on. "What do you want, by the way?"

"What's that mean?"

"You get to know me and you'll find I don't say a whole lot of shit I don't mean, so it means exactly what I said. What do you want to happen when I drop you off at Hugh's?"

"To get him to answer for what his brother did."

"And what if the answer is 'Fuck you'?" Apparently they hadn't thought of that. "I've seen it happen before."

"Then maybe I shoot his ass."

"Okay, now we're talking. That's a plan."

Harrison seemed confused by Calvin's lack of fear. "Hey, shut the hell up. Just get us there."

"You got the gun, you're the boss." Calvin inched down on the gas, pushing the car slowly up over seventy.

"You got any tunes?" Conrad asked from behind. "I could go for some tunes."

"I like to focus on the road while I drive," Calvin said.

Harrison lifted the gun. "Put on the damn radio. Play the man a song."

Calvin pressed harder on the accelerator. The dial inched past eighty.

"You got any requests?"

"Just some music, man." Conrad spoke like he needed a song the way a drunk needs a bottle.

"I think there's a country station I can usually get out of Des Moines." Calvin moved the needle over ninety. Harrison started to take notice.

"Hey, slow down, man."

"I thought you were in a rush to ask Hugh about this mess?" Calvin didn't try to hide it anymore. He brought the pedal to the floor and the Demon moved over one hundred.

Harrison put a hand on the dashboard, fixing himself to the seat. The lap belt remained unlatched. His gun stayed aimed at Calvin's gut. Up ahead twin silos blinked with red lights to warn any low flying airplanes, but to Calvin they looked like two eyes.

"I said slow it down." Harrison waved the gun as if Calvin might have forgotten it was there between them.

"Shit, Harrison. This bastard is gonna run us off in a ditch."

"Relax, boys. I got this," Calvin said. "Now how about those tunes."

He lifted a hand off the wheel and reached for a dial on the dash. Ahead of them the highway went black.

"Shit," Calvin said in mock dismay. "Wrong button."

"Turn on the goddamn lights," Conrad squealed from the back.

"Put 'em back on, man," Harrison said. Calvin knew he'd be waving the gun around, even though the car was dark now.

"I got it, I got it." The radio clicked on and Calvin cranked the knob as far right as it would turn. The speakers pounded and rattled to the sound of Conway Twitty and Loretta Lynn singing *After the Fire is Gone*, though the way it distorted you'd think they were caught in the middle of the fire.

Harrison had to shout, "Hey," just to be heard over the crackling country song.

"One thing, Harrison," Calvin said as he came even with the twin silos. "I ain't your fucking chauffeur."

Calvin cut the wheel left, lifted his foot off the gas and slid the car toward a dirt access road leading to the silos. In the darkness of the cabin he reached over Harrison's body and pulled his door handle. Harrison was already pressed tight against the door from the g-force of the sudden turn. Released, the door whipped open and the night sucked Harrison out into the blackness.

Calvin turned the wheels into the skid, keeping the back end from drifting too far. The dirt of the farm road made it easier on him and let the car slide with little effort. He got the car facing forward again and the swinging of the body back to straight slammed the door on the empty passenger seat. He pressed on toward the silos.

"What the fuck?" Conrad spit on the back of Calvin's neck as he spoke in a hoarse shout over the music.

Calvin tuned him out and flicked the lights back on. He gripped the wheel tight between his fists and wrestled the car to stay true, a harder task on the uneven road. He could hear his passenger rolling around the backseat like a bag of groceries. He caught glimpses in the rearview of Conrad's flailing body.

Calvin turned for the silos, knowing there would be smooth ground all around the structure. He kept the Demon near seventy as he circled the silos and got going back toward the two lane pavement.

"Stop this goddamn car."

Calvin felt the cold steel of Conrad's gun at the back of his neck. He reached forward and pressed the stereo off. The hungry thunder of the engine filled the space.

"I said stop, motherfucker."

"You really want to shoot the driver of a car going over eighty? What happens next?"

Conrad gave the question some thought.

"You shoot me," Calvin said. "We both die, only when the car rolls and traps you inside as it crushes you in a twist of metal or maybe when it catches fire and you can't get out, I'll already be dead since you shot me in the fucking head without thinking about it first. Kinda like when you and your boy decided to go visit Hugh Stanley without a goddamn plan."

Calvin steered back onto the blacktop, lights flashing over the broken and crawling figure of Harrison moving on all fours and leaving a trail of blood as he felt his way in the dark.

"You go back and get him," Conrad said, leaning forward and pressing the gun harder into Calvin's neck. Calvin had guns pulled on him before. They didn't frighten him the way the men usually wanted, especially if he was driving. At the control of a two thousand pound death machine, Calvin McGraw felt nearly invincible. Some people took a little more convincing was all.

"You wanna go back and get him?"

"I said do it, asshole."

Calvin shook his head. "No plan."

He stomped on the brake. The car gripped the asphalt and the nose dove forward. Conrad tipped and Calvin grabbed him with both hands, hauled him forward over his shoulder and slammed him into the dashboard. The gun clattered to the floor. Conrad started screaming about his broken nose.

Calvin got both hands back on the wheel and guided the car to a stop amid the stench of burning tires. He got out, walked to the passenger side and opened the door. Conrad came tumbling out, hitting his head on the highway. Calvin, surging with adrenaline, lifted the man by the back of his shirt and put his head in between the door and the body of the car. He slammed the door on Conrad's head.

"You see? I had a plan."

He slammed again. Conrad went limp—passed out. Calvin dragged him to the back bumper and muscled him into the trunk. He'd be feeling the soreness from the workout tomorrow.

Calvin spun the car back toward the farm house. He'd never picked up his cargo.

When he pulled to a stop in front of the farm house, Kirby stood on the porch, grinning.

Calvin had to shake his head. He hadn't held out much

hope, but there was that chance and seeing Kirby alive meant the other man was dead—probably in some spectacular way.

Calvin opened the trunk and said, "What do you want to do with him?"

"Get him inside. See how he likes being tied to a goddamn chair for a while."

"You're not gonna kill him?"

"Someone has to be here to tell the tale."

"Shit, Kirby, I thought you'd do it just for the ear."

"Oh, I'm still gonna take his ear." Kirby's smile went wider.

Calvin stayed out by the car—his domain—while Kirby worked inside. Just what he'd seen when he helped Kirby get Conrad inside was enough nightmare fuel for a year. However he'd gotten away from the remaining man at the house, the fool had suffered the full wrath of Kirby's anger for being tied up and abused. The kitchen had been remodeled in red.

When Kirby came out he was dropping a fresh ear into the front pocket on his jacket, a pocket that already appeared to be full.

"You got any tunes?" Kirby asked once they got rolling.

"Whatever you say," Calvin said. He put on the radio at a reasonable volume and let Kirby pick the station.

When Calvin saw the silo lights ahead he kept an eye out for any movement in the headlights. He spotted Harrison on the shoulder, still on all fours and treading softly on his right arm. Cal slowed the car until they were parallel to him. Kirby rolled down his window.

"Nebraska's the other way, shithead." Harrison looked up at the car. Both his eyes were nearly swollen shut. His upper lip was fat and bruised. He cradled his right arm and the wrist looked badly broken.

"If you ever do get back there," Kirby said. "You tell Cantrell to stay on his side of the corn field, you dig?"

Calvin punched the accelerator and the Demon growled away into the night.

7

Webb remembered the first time he went on a run with his father. He was ten. They drove a pickup with twelve cases of corn liquor in the back. They delivered it to a juke joint on the banks of the Mississippi, a plywood and sheet metal lean-to that looked like the river had dumped it on the shore and would sweep it away again any minute.

Webb hung out by the truck as Calvin instructed two men from the bar where to put the liquor. The sounds of live blues came through the loose walls of the juke and got louder each time the back door would open.

"Hey, man," one of the juke joint workers, Cyrus, said. "This is quite a change—a whitey comin' in through the back door." He laughed and Calvin laughed with him. Webb didn't get the joke, but he saw the camaraderie. He saw two outlaw men doing their business. He wanted to be a part of that club and listen to that music all night long.

"Hey, McGraw," Cyrus said. "You givin' rides tonight?"

Calvin cracked a sly grin, looked out over the river and said, "I might could do a few rounds."

Cyrus hollered and slapped his hands together then ran inside and came out with a long length of rope tied to the end of a plank of wood. Calvin told Webb to get up in the truck as he tied the rope onto the trailer hitch and pulled into a set of ruts running alongside the river. Cyrus took the wood plank and set it down in a few inches of water, took up the rope slack in his hand and said, "Hit it."

Calvin gunned the engine and they took off in a spray of river mud. As Calvin gained speed down the mud path next to the river, the wood plank skimmed the surface of the water and Cyrus let out another whoop as he rode the plank like a skipping stone across the Mississippi.

They drove that muddy path five more times that night and by the time they were done, Webb's sides ached from laughing.

Eastern Missouri rolled steeper with hills and thickened with trees the deeper Webb traveled into her. He'd turned off the exit and watched each road sign he passed looking for clues about the address he sought. Thirty minutes of searching turned up his number.

Webb let the Mercury rest as he walked to the door of an ordinary suburban home. He stood on the porch for a while feeling bad about the late hour and wondering if he should knock, when the door opened and a long-haired man in a denim shirt and a thick beard stared back at him.

"You the Stanley man?"

"Yep."

The beard turned without a word and went back into the shadows of the house. When he returned a few seconds later there was a girl with him, her arm clenched tight in his fist.

"Here she is."

He pushed the girl forward at Webb. She had a single shoulder bag in off white macrame, flared jeans nearly threadbare in the knees and a flower print top that opened wide at the neck nearly revealing her ample breasts. Couldn't have been more than twenty. Her hair was cut in a short boy cut that reminded Webb of Goldie Hawn on *Laugh-In*. He'd never seen a girl with short cut hair like that in person, only in magazines and on TV. Webb needed a minute to take in how attractive she was. By the time he snapped out of it, the door was almost closed in his face.

"Hey, you got a beer or something? I've been driving a long time."

The beard gave him an unsure look, then said, "Wait here."

The girl clutched her bag to her chest like it might save her from drowning. Her eyes reminded him of some alley cats he'd seen. Always on the lookout, suspicious of everything.

He could hear his father's voice in the back of his mind. Pick up the cargo, deliver the cargo. That's all. It doesn't matter what's in the package. But a person was different, right?

"Pretty shitty way to make a living," she said. Webb wasn't sure if she meant him or herself.

The beard appeared back at the door with two cans of Pabst. He handed one to Webb who thanked him and held out one to the girl. She slapped it out of his hand and it hit the concrete porch, split open on the side and a thin spray of beer spouted onto the house.

"Goddamn it, Joni. I sure am glad you're not my problem anymore."

"Fuck you, Spider." She spit in his direction.

The beard raised a hand like he might slap her. Webb grabbed his wrist and held it above the beard's head. They traded unblinking stares for a moment, then Spider seemed to decide it wasn't worth the hassle.

"Yeah, well, she's your trouble now." Spider tore his arm free and shut the door on them.

Webb stood on the porch listening to the beer can run out of pressure and slow its hissing until the can rolled off the top step and landed in the grass.

"I suppose you want me to thank you or some shit," Joni said.

"No."

"Well, good. 'Cause I'm not. What you're doing is awful. I don't wanna go, you know. I don't wanna see that man again. You know what he's gonna do to me, right?"

Webb didn't know, and didn't want to. He cracked the pull top on his beer, tossed the ring into the grass by his buddy and took a long swig.

"Let's go," he said.

"What if I refuse?"

Webb hadn't counted on that. Didn't know what to say. His silence served as a warning to her. Whatever went unsaid was worse in her imagination than anything he could have told her so she slung the bag over her shoulder and started down the steps. "Let's get this over with."

He drank the rest of the beer, crushed the can in his fist and dropped it on the lawn then turned to catch up to Joni who was already halfway to the car.

"What the shit is this?" She looked over the car, peering the window at the missing backseat.

"It's a car."

"It's a pice of junk."

"It's a Mercury Cougar Eliminator with a Boss 429 V8 under the hood."

"Yeah, well, still a piece of junk."

Webb wrinkled his face at her. "Was that guy right? Am I gonna have trouble with you?"

She thrust out a hip sideways, waited for him to open her door. "As much as I can give you."

Webb shook his head and lifted one corner of his mouth in a half grin. He walked away from her, got behind the wheel and let her open her own damn door. When his door shut she took off running. Webb scrambled to get out. By the time he stood she was across the lawn and headed into the neighbor's yard. He ran.

After all that driving it felt good to stretch his legs, but he hadn't planned to do it this way. Joni's high heeled boots made it difficult moving across grass damp with midnight dew. He caught her before she made it to the next yard. He didn't know what to do so he tackled her from behind.

They rolled and he came up on top of her, the macrame bag between them, her breasts threatening to spill out of her top.

"Careful, boy, a ride ain't free y'know."

Webb felt his cheeks blush. He rolled off and hauled her to her feet. Both their jeans were grass stained and they each fought to catch their breath. As Webb marched her back to the car he thought how nice it was that bundles of dope or cases of hooch didn't talk and couldn't run.

8

Calvin came into Hugh's office like a gunslinger into a saloon.

"This is bullshit, Hugh. I've got half a mind to quit."

"You've had half a mind to quit ever since I met you, McGraw."

"Yeah, well, this time it's the other half."

Hugh stood and went to his wet bar. "You've been shot at before."

"It's different when it's cops. They're not looking to kill. They want an arrest, not a funeral." Hugh handed Calvin a straight whiskey. "This shit? With a guy like Cantrell and his crew? This is gonna end bad and that's not even taking into account the way it started."

"Relax, Cal. Take a drink."

Calvin studied the tumbler in his hand. "Don't you have any beer?"

Hugh chuckled, downed his own glass, and called his assistant to run and get them a few cold beers.

"Kirby told me what you did out there, Cal. How you stopped them coming after me. I'm obliged."

Calvin didn't take to compliments or praise very well. "What was I gonna do, drive up to your front door and ring the bell like Avon calling?"

"Point is, Cal, I always knew you were good at driving, but you're proving yourself very adept at taking out problems in the form of our enemies."

"I didn't take nobody out. I don't do that. I just gave 'em a little shove out of my damn car. I don't kill for you, Hugh. You know that."

"Sounds like right then you'd have been killing for yourself."

"If that matter comes up I won't hesitate to protect me and mine. But this wasn't that."

"Either way," Hugh sat back down in his big leather chair. "I thank you."

A soft knock on the door was followed by a buxom blonde with an armload of beer cans.

"Thanks, Dottie," Hugh said.

She set the beers on the bar and left with a healthy shake to her hips like she was advertising the space for rent. Hugh took a long, admiring look.

Calvin cracked a beer. "Tell me this is gonna be okay."

"There needs to be a response," Hugh said. "But we'll handle it."

"All I do is drive. Don't get any fancy ideas."

"I know, Cal. Don't worry."

Calvin finished his beer in three massive gulps. "I gotta get some sleep."

"Sounds good. Hey, will you send in Dottie for me when you head out."

Hugh was loosening his tie. Calvin knew what that meant. Hugh planned on renting a little space on that billboard she was shaking around.

Out front he smelled the smoke first. Nancy's sandpaper purr came next.

"You look like you need to relax."

Vic had been nowhere to be seen tonight. Hugh's secretary probably already had a mouthful. Kirby was off organizing his ears somewhere. Everyone in the Stanley clan doing their best to relax after a long and stressful day, and here was Nancy, offering herself to Calvin again.

"Leave me alone, Nancy."

She blew smoke into the night. "See you in your dreams, lover."

Calvin turned away from her, anxious to get home to his wife.

The next morning nobody called. Calvin was looking at a day all to himself. He and Dorothy grilled hot dogs for lunch, talked about going to see a movie at the Englert Theatre, stayed home instead and worked a thousand piece puzzle of Mount Rushmore.

He hadn't told her about his close call at the farm house. No need to worry her. He knew she held a lot inside and carried a knot of worry in her gut every time he stepped out on a job. Certainly wasn't worth spoiling a perfectly quaint Midwestern day.

"Are we boring?" Calvin asked.

"And proud of it." Dorothy picked out an edge piece of blue sky.

"I mean it."

She lifted her eyes from the puzzle. "Calvin McGraw, you spend half your life moving faster than the law allows. What's so bad about slowing life down once in a while? Maybe even parking it in the garage."

Calvin smiled. "Oh, I'd like to park it in your garage." He winked at her.

"Calvin, you know your dumb jokes are no way to get me in the mood."

"It's all I got. I traded my good looks to the devil himself to get a beautiful girl to fall for me."

Dorothy smiled and set down her piece of sky. "Now, that's more like it."

**

Webb's day started slow.

She was late getting up, snoring like a blackout drunk until he kicked her hard enough on her legs so she finally woke up. Then she spent a full hour in the shower until Webb was sure as anything the motel would run out of hot water. Twice he got up and went around back to check the window and make sure she hadn't snuck out. While there, he felt an obligation to make sure she was inside and if that meant taking a gander through the frosted glass and steam smeared window to see blurry movement and a myopic outline of Joni's naked body then so be it.

She was in there all right. A fuzzy outline had never looked so good.

Webb scolded himself for thinking of her as anything but cargo. He banged on the bathroom door. "I'm gonna go check out. When I get back you'd better be ready to roll. You hear me?"

No response, only the steady rush of the shower.

When he got back she was out and standing in the center of the room with a towel wrapped around her, creating a perilously short mini dress. Webb turned away from her on instinct to protect her privacy.

Her tone hadn't improved even after the long shower. "I only got the one set of clothes, y'know?"

"Just put on what you had on yesterday. It doesn't matter."

"That's what I had on the day before that, too. I need something new."

"Like hell you do, we gotta get going."

"You really want to deliver me to Mr. Stanley smelling like day three of Woodstock?"

She had a point. "Well, I'm not taking you out like that."

"I'll get dressed, but first stop is a clothes store."

"It's ten 'til noon already."

"So they'll be open."

Webb gave in. He knew his dad would be disappointed, but her point about Hugh was solid. It would be like delivering damaged goods, and that's a no-no.

"Get dressed fast at least."

"You gonna turn around or do I charge you ten bucks for the show?"

Webb turned to face the door. Joni's mocking laughter stung at his back.

Calvin got the call around two o'clock when his mind was a thousand miles away from work and the Stanleys. He'd been contemplating a phone call to Marshall Pruitt all day, but wasn't sure what he'd say.

It wasn't unusual to go days or even weeks between jobs. His was a specialty skill. But now it seemed like Calvin had stepped knee deep in whatever pile of shit was building between Iowa and Nebraska in a turf war for the saddest plot of criminal empire in America. Miles and miles of corn fields spread thick with manure. A stretch of land literally covered in bullshit.

"Gotta go in," he told Dorothy.

She sighed, but she knew the drill. "Running you ragged these days."

He kept a tight lip. "Yeah."

She waited for any elaboration, but none came. "Want to take a coffee with you?"

"Nah, I'll be okay."

Not knowing what was in store for the night he knew was harder on his wife than on himself. But if Dorothy felt any fears, she kept them well hid.

"You be safe out there."

"Will do."

Calvin kissed her gently on the lips and clutched his keys in hand out the door.

When the rumble of the V8 had faded, Dorothy went to the linen closet and reached behind the towels. She withdrew the bottle of Kentucky bourbon and noticed the level had dropped below the label. One drink. One double to steel her resolve. It kept the thoughts at bay without getting her drunk. It slowed her heartbeat without putting her to sleep. Calvin wouldn't mind even if he knew. She wasn't quite sure why she kept it hidden, just that she didn't want him to worry about her worrying.

She replaced the bottle and went to the freezer next. She took out the quart of ice cream and started on phase two of the ritual. Calvin hadn't noticed the few extra pounds she had put on or if he had he was a gentleman and hadn't said anything. She figured if her face filled out a bit it might hid the lines of worry before they carved too deep.

Calvin walked in on an argument between Hugh and Vic. Hugh remained anchored behind his desk, a cigar left smoldering in an ashtray while Vic paced the room like the floor was hot coals.

"We need to make room for it in our business model," Vic said.

"Business model? Where did you read that shit? 'Cause I know you're not smart enough for that on your own."

"If we don't start moving some coke, Cantrell's gonna own it from the rockies to Appalachia. And he's offering us a partnership—"

"He's offering us to be his servant boys. It's cheap shit up from where? Mexico? Colombia? Who the fuck knows what's in it?"

"The people snorting it don't give a shit."

"I do. We run a quality product ever since your grandpa and mine cooked shine out of a copper still on Westlake Mountain."

Vic pounded a fist into the palm of his other hand. "You're leaving money on the table, Hugh."

Hugh's voice raised in volume, but dropped an octave. "I don't work for nobody else. They want us to distribute? And for what? A cut? We have to hand off fifty-sixty percent to them when it's *our* guys on the street corners?" He motioned to Calvin. "*Our* guys moving the shit around? No way. I'm working on getting some from domestic sources. There's a guy in Chicago who says he can start production."

"It'll be too late," Vic said, pleading. "Cantrell's got shit here and now. He's ready to move and he don't want to wait."

"You know a lot about this shit, huh?"

Vic looked away from his brother's accusing stare. "I'm trying to build our business here, Hugh."

"All this deal will do is build his. We do it right. We wait. And we let him know he's not welcome here."

Vic rubbed the tip of his nose. He couldn't stand it any more. The stress was too much and he needed a line.

"This is horse shit." He brushed past Calvin and slammed the door.

"We need to strike back." Hugh Stanley lifted the cigar and puffed it back to life as he cooled in his leather chair and laid out the plan for Calvin.

"I notice," Calvin said, "that you never leave this office, yet you have no problem sending the rest of us out in battle."

"That's exactly it, Cal. I'm like a general. I have to be here to coordinate the troops."

"Going about as well as it's going in Vietnam, I'd say."

Calvin knew he'd crossed a line, or at least stepped on it. Hugh didn't like to talk about the war since his brother, Ennis – third in line between Vic and Kirby – died there.

"We'll win that," Hugh said. "And we'll win this, too." He chugged smoke like MacArthur overlooking Midway.

"Hugh, I didn't mean to—"

"Just remember your job around here, McGraw."

It was meant to put Calvin in his place, but he rarely stayed where others wanted him to be.

"I'm trying. And last I recall, I wasn't on the front lines rushing us into battle."

Hugh set the cigar down. "Dammit, Cal, let's not fight about this shit. We're on the same side. I need you and you know why I need you. You got experience. You got nerve.

61

You've done too good recently for me not to have you along. I got a crew full of young guys with a lot of piss and vinegar, but they're not the sharpest tools in the shed. You got street smarts. Life experience. Twenty plus years in this life. And all I need you to do is drive."

"So I just deliver this crew to the Cantrell house outside of Ames? I wait for them to, what, clear it out?"

"It's an outpost a little too close for comfort."

"All I do is deliver them and bring them back."

"That's all. Keep your head on a swivel and be ready to bust out of there if they need it."

"Why do I feel like I'm a pilot on the Enola Gay?"

"Because you're doing the right thing to end this war."

Hugh picked up his cigar again, puffed it until it glowed red, then leaned back in his chair.

9

Near the river, in a flat industrial square made of brick, a half dozen men were about to die. They made the mistake of taking a job as criminals and as such they followed orders and set up shop in a state not their own. Calvin crossed a small bridge, saw the cluster of abandoned storage facilities and one time factories, and wished these kids had just stayed home in Nebraska.

In his line of work, Calvin rarely had to confront death or violence. He drove for the thrill of it. Getting chased by cops was just another burst of adrenalin. A Mountain Dew straight to the heart. He could drive a truck but there was no thrill there. He could do deliveries of flowers or dry cleaning or the U.S. mail—but come on, they couldn't compare to outlaw driving.

Stock Car racing? Sure, as long as you liked being beholden to a sponsor, wearing ties like Pruitt and as long as you really liked only turning left. Fucking pussies.

No, Calvin inherited the bug from his dad and he'd passed it down to Webb. It was in their blood like nitrous. Hell, it didn't even feel like breaking the law most times.

This wasn't one of those times.

He toted five men with him in a long station wagon that rode like mush and had the pickup of a broke leg mule. He didn't like such an oversized car but the job wouldn't do with only three men that could fit into one of his muscle cars, and Calvin could coax miracles of burnt rubber from the most unassuming of cars.

The only one he'd bothered to learn his name was the man next to him up front. Willie wore his hair slicked back on his head like he'd fallen into a pit of mud. He wore a tight necklace of tiny shells and a camouflage jacket that spoke of his time in Nam. Hiring veterans was standard practice for the Stanleys. They'd already been trained to kill, plus it reminded them of Ennis in a good way.

Calvin parked a decent way away and all five men racked shells into the chambers of their wide assortment of guns.

"Keep it running," Willie said.

"I know how it's done."

Once he heard the first shots fired, Calvin would pull the wagon closer to the building so the men wouldn't have to make it as far for the getaway. The plan was to leave the place stacked with more bodies than a city morgue and with nobody chasing them, but plans always change. Calvin was being paid to anticipate the changes.

Willie turned to address the troops. "Everyone good? Remember to bring your balls with you, 'cause you're gonna need 'em."

One of the men in the way back gave a "Hoo-rah!" and Calvin wondered if they'd served together.

"Let's take out this Cantrell scum."

Three doors and the back hatch all sprung open at once and the quintet of men hustled across the broken asphalt lot toward the brick building. Calvin watched them go in his side mirror, then his rearview. They paused outside the door and waited on Willie's command. He gave a hand signal and they went in. The shots started almost immediately.

Calvin put the wagon into reverse and eased it close to the door where the men had entered. The sound of gunfire was thick and varied. Thirty-eights, forty-fives, a shotgun. Death lay beyond that door.

He felt a small pang of guilt for sitting outside in relative safety. The truth was if Webb wanted to sign up to one of the Stanley's death crews, Calvin would forbid it. He didn't want his son to cross the line from outlaw to criminal. From driver to killer. Not for money, anyway.

In Calvin's eyes, you killed a man you'd better have a damn good reason and you'd better know the man first. You looked him in the eye. You told him what you came to do, then you did it.

He'd done it. He didn't like it, but he'd finished the job. Stared straight into the man's eyes and explained his reasons. It wasn't so much the sound of gunfire but the smell of a recently fired gun that brought it all back. He knew he'd have five men with sizzling guns getting in his car soon and he'd have to smell it all the way home, haunting him like a ghost who can't find peace.

There came a lull in the shooting. A good sign. Nobody had been sure how many men they'd encounter inside. Maybe they were all dead already. Calvin was too much a realist to think none of his crew had taken a hit. A beater like this wagon though? Bleed all you want on it. It's gonna get torched after this job anyway.

If he hadn't looked up at the right moment, Calvin might

not have seen the guy. On the second floor, he watched as feet came backward through a small side window. The rest of the man slithered out and paused while he hung there with fingers clutched to the window frame, his legs twenty feet above the ground.

He hadn't broken the window and he was being quiet. He sure didn't look like one of the men Calvin had driven up there, but he was honest with himself enough to know that if it was one of the guys sitting in the way back, he couldn't pick them out of a lineup.

The man swayed there for a long moment, thinking about the fall. Calvin could see him trying to get his eyes to look down, but with his face to the brick and his arms stretched to their limit, he had a hard time of it.

A pop of gunfire here and there let Calvin know they were sweeping the rest of the building, but still no one had come outside and Calvin was watching one of the Cantrell men escape.

The man let go, either on purpose or his fingers gave out. He dropped, scraping along the rough brick surface of the building. He landed on a pile of broken pallets overgrown with tall weeds sprouting between the cracked slats.

Calvin watched with interest as the pile of debris sat motionless. Dead or just knocked out? He couldn't get out to go see. Rule number one was never leave the vehicle. Even with this fascinating turn of events playing out in front of him like a TV show, he instinctively kept his hands at ten and two.

The pile moved. A head poked out like a gopher from a hole. This gopher bled down his face, probably from scraping the bricks on the way down. He saw no trouble, made no notice of the wagon, and took off running across the lot with a severe limp in his left leg.

Calvin hopped on his seat like a kid who needed to pee. All he could do was watch the enemy slip away. He debated honking the horn, but what if the limper still had his gun?

"Come on, come on, come on." Calvin slapped the steering wheel, rocking in his seat with pent-up energy. A single shot came from the warehouse.

Calvin watched the man drag his left leg over the asphalt, cracked and sprouting with dry brown weeds. He seemed to be heading for another squat brick building on the other side. Beyond that lay a train yard a good quarter mile from there, or if he turned right—the river.

Could be the guy was a champion swimmer, but Calvin doubted it.

He turned back to the building, willing someone to come out the door.

"Hurry up, damn it."

The doorway stayed empty.

It sure as hell sounded like they'd gotten them all. Unless the Cantrell's got the Stanleys too. Calvin had to speculate that limping man was the only one left alive.

But if his crew had gotten all of them, then there would be no penalty for not being there when they emerged. He could go hunt down the gimp and save an embarrassing and potentially dangerous mistake.

What if he caught up to him? Then what? He was unarmed and unwilling to kill an already wounded man he'd never seen before. His world was behind the wheel, not in the trenches, although it felt like the two were rapidly becoming the same space.

Calvin watched the man disappear behind the far brick

building. Gone for good, perhaps.

"Shit, shit, shit." He pounded the dash and the plastic cover popped off the clock face. Cheap-ass car.

Movement to his right caught his eye. Willie stepped out of the building putting a cigarette to his lips and smiling at a joke someone told. Calvin kicked open the passenger door.

"Get in."

Willie saw the serious look on Calvin's face and double timed it to the car. Before he had the door shut, Calvin was moving. The other men came spilling out of the building and shouting, "What the fuck?"

So did Willie. "What the fuck?"

"How are you on ammo?"

"Huh? I ran out my clip."

"Then load another."

"What for?"

"Got a runner."

Willie turned eyes forward. "Where?"

"Came out the second floor window. Went around that building there."

Calvin pointed where the nose of the car aimed. The soft shocks bounced over the uneven cracks in the asphalt as Calvin pushed the wagon over fifty.

He skidded tires around the corner of the building. Ahead he saw the gimp's head jerk up at the sound. He moved like he'd seen a bullet aimed his way. Willie saw him too.

"I'll be a son of a..."

Calvin flattened the pedal, the hearty engine gave a deep throated rumble. Willie had his gun out. Ahead of them the gimp moved as fast as his broken leg would allow. Each step with his right was followed by a wide swing of his left leg.

When he turned over his shoulder to check the progress of the approaching car, Calvin could see the blood smeared down his face.

He seemed to be headed for the river. The train yard was too far and they both knew it. But there stood a good three hundred yards of open parking lot between the gimp and the riverbank. And only about three hundred and fifty for Calvin.

"Ram him," Willie said. "Just plow the fucker over."

"Not my job," Calvin said. "I don't kill them. Just deliver you to do it."

"The fuck is that about?"

"I'm the goddamn driver. That's all."

Calvin skidded to a stop, tires tearing through the sprouting weeds. Willie pitched forward, never having put on his belt.

"There you go," Calvin said. "Easy shot."

Willie got out and marched toward the retreating gimp with his gun outstretched before him. He fired once. Missed. The gimp felt the shot pound into the ground only a foot or two away. He zigged, should have zagged. He came down on his busted left leg and collapsed with a holler.

Calvin turned away. He heard the final shot a few seconds later.

10

Webb's day didn't go well. Joni took her sweet time at breakfast, sending the waitress away three times for more coffee before she even ordered real food. And after her eggs were sopped up on a greasy biscuit, she wouldn't budge from the booth until she'd smoked up four cigarettes.

Webb grew impatient but the last thing he needed was a scene in a public place. As soon as they entered the vinyl and Formica restaurant he regretted it. She had every reason to start crying rape or kidnapping. Something about Webb being from the Stanley crew kept her in line. Maybe she knew if she got away there would be a replacement to come along only days later and bring her back to Iowa, or maybe she thought Webb might just shoot her where she stood.

In Joni's head, she thought the getting shot option might not be so bad.

She asked the waitress when she brought their change, "Is there, like, a shopping mall around here or something? Some place a gal can get a change of clothes?"

"Well, now," the waitress said, thinking. "You might could try Buck's Department store. That's out off the main road just north of here. They got real nice dresses and such."

She wore a uniform so it was hard to tell the waitress's style, but judging by the high beehive hairdo and pancake makeup trying to plaster in all the wrinkles in her north-of-forty face, it was a safe bet she and Joni didn't share the same taste in clothes.

Still, Joni smiled and said, "Thank you." When the waitress left with a smile and an armload of dirty dishes, Joni turned to Webb and said, "You give her a nice big tip."

Webb sighed and added another dollar to the pile he left behind.

Out in the car Joni said, "So let's go south and see what's what."

"She said north."

"I'm not going to no department store. Not one that she shops at. No fucking way."

"Then why did you ask?"

"I asked about a shopping mall. Some place with a lot of stores."

"How much are you gonna buy? We'll be home in a few hours."

She pursed her lips at him. "So I only need one more outfit because why? When I get there they're gonna shoot me? Do you know something I don't know?"

"No one's gonna shoot you." *At least I don't think so*, Webb thought. "But don't you think Hugh's gonna—Mr. Stanley is going to buy you some new clothes once you're home?"

"That's not my home. Don't you say that shit again. And he *is* buying me new clothes because you're gonna pay. Now go south."

Webb started the car. "I know what you're doing."

"And what's that, Einstein?"

71

"You're stalling. You're taking your sweet time because you don't want to go back. You're taking us south when we need to be going north." He looked at her with a grin. "I see what you're up to."

"You're still gonna take me."

"You think so, huh?"

"Yeah. 'Cause if you take me to the mall I'll show you my tits."

She lifted her T-shirt and flashed her braless breasts. They bounced twice from the action of her shirt lifting from below and Webb lost his attempt to look away. He saw her near perfect B cups right there in his front seat. She lowered her shirt while he was still in stunned silence.

"So let's go," she said.

"Now, hold on—"

"I already showed them to you. You can't go back on a deal now."

"I didn't agree to any deal. You said it and fast as lightning your tits were out. I didn't have a choice."

"You didn't have to look."

Webb could see arguing would only prolong the delays, so he dropped the car in gear and sped away with a rooster tail of gravel spitting from the rear tires.

Joni liked this little pushover. If they met in another circumstance she thought she'd think he was groovy. He made a funny face when he was frustrated—like he did right then turning south on the main road out of town, away from Iowa looming over them on the horizon.

She decided then that she wouldn't kill him. The pen knife in her bag would take some work to kill anyone, but she'd been prepared to do it if need be. She'd go for the throat. That's how she did it in her mind every time she imagined using it. She'd stab, make it dig deep and then turn the blade and drag it out the other side. If she did it right, sunk the blade in deep enough, she could kill someone with one sweep of her wrist.

But not Webb. Not today. Nah. He was kinda cute. Needed to grow his hair out some more. And learn to play tunes in the car. The silence was getting on her nerves. But, yeah, she liked him enough not to kill him.

***

The station wagon sat in a dark parking lot beside a liquor store, engine running.

One of them had been hit in the leg. Calvin listened to the men in back discussing the best way to keep the wound wrapped until they could get to proper medical help. The man who'd been hit was toughing it out and begging off any help.

Calvin watched Willie in the phone booth ahead. They'd stopped to put in a call after the job. Willie had been inside the glass booth for ten minutes already, his arms gesturing wildly as he recounted the action.

"I said I'm fine, man," the wounded man said. "Quit being a bitch and leave me be."

"It was the stubby little one who did it. I saw him."

"Yeah, I got that motherfucker. Don't you worry, chief. He paid for what he done to you."

Calvin listened and thought, *what he did was defend himself when you all came charging in loaded for bear.* He'd thought many times over the years that who the bad guy was really depended on what side of the door you're on. He also knew Cantrell started this shit. He'd been there to witness the first shot, and it cost Bruce more than a flesh wound.

Willie hung up and came jogging back to the car. He slid into the passenger seat and said to Calvin, "He wants to see you."

"When? Tonight?"

"Yeah."

"Aw, come on, man. I want to go home and get some sleep."

"The man said it was important. Wants you to come to the house."

"Shit." Calvin didn't get summoned to Hugh's personal home often. Nobody did. That meant real news. "All right. Let me drop you guys at Doc Moller's place."

"He knows we're coming."

Calvin pointed a thumb over his shoulder. "Your boy there thinks he doesn't even need a doctor."

"That boy is stupid. Took some shrapnel in Nam and didn't tell nobody for three days until it got infected. Had to cut out a hunk of his back. Got a big ol nasty scar there now. Got him sent home, though."

"Maybe not so stupid after all."

Willie smiled. "Maybe not." He turned to his troops. "Hey, I'm gonna go in and get a bottle. Who wants what?"

All four men gave different answers. Willie said, "I'll get a fifth of something dark, something clear and some tequila for me. Cal, what do you want?"

"Nothing for me." He thought about his meeting. "Know what? Get me a beer. I'll save it for later."

11

Calvin exchanged the wagon for his Dodge Demon and parked at the curb outside Hugh Stanley's house on Raven street. The name always brought to mind a dark black bird sitting on his shoulder whispering "Nevermore".

He knocked on Hugh's door, amazed at the simplicity of the house. Hugh wasn't trying to draw attention. He lived like all the salesmen, car dealers, plumbers and schoolteachers on the street beside him. Nothing to say *I run a criminal empire*. It made Calvin think what he'd suspected for years about the Stanley's—that they made about as much profit from their lifestyle as someone who owned a moderately popular pizza joint, maybe with three or four locations in the county. Calvin certainly wasn't getting rich from the life, and it didn't seem like the Stanley's were either.

Beat working for a living, though.

A muscle bound bodyguard answered the door.

"He's next door."

"They told me to come here."

"He's with Vic. Said for you to go on over."

Great. Victor Stanley lived next door.

Calvin wasn't thrilled about going to Vic's. If both brothers were there it meant a more serious meeting and with the way things had been going of late, bad news was coming.

He crossed the lawn to Vic's front door. Vic made at least an attempt at looking lavish. Twin Greek-inspired statues flanked the door. Topless Goddesses holding urns and sheaves of wheat. They were done in faux marble, but it was wearing down to the plaster in places likes the tip of one girl's nose and the pointed ends of their nipples. They weren't fooling anybody.

Calvin was welcomed inside to a house decorated in gold trimmings and oversized reproductions of Renaissance art. Nancy's decorating in full effect and it came off as cheap and gaudy as her.

Hugh and Victor were in the den. Calvin was ushered inside. The air hung heavy with cigar smoke and the room was stifling and hot. Hugh sat in a high backed leather armchair while Victor stood immediately and went to the wet bar.

"Hiya, Cal. What can I get you?"

"Nothing, thanks." Calvin had left his beer warming in the Demon. A drink implied he was there to stay for a while. He wanted to get out fast.

"Good work tonight," Hugh said.

"Really good," Vic added. "We heard all about it."

"Something tells me the way Willie described it might be a bit more like a movie than what really happened."

"Five guys went in, five guys came out. That's what counts. And you didn't let that little rat bastard get away. Sneaky fuck."

Calvin wasn't interested in rehashing the day. "It's been a long one. You wanted to see me about something other than a stroke job?"

Hugh traded a look with Vic. "Have a seat, Cal."

"I've been sitting from here to Ames and back. I'll stand."

Vic bounced himself down on a short couch, nearly spilling his double scotch rocks. On the glass coffee table Calvin saw a small bone-inlaid box on top of a mirrored tray. Vic's coke stash. One of them, anyway. He'd never dare bust out a line in front of Hugh, but it made Calvin wonder if Vic paid wholesale for the stuff or if he got it pre-cut at a five finger discount. After what he'd overheard of their argument, he knew they weren't moving coke these days, not regularly anyway. Vic had some other supplier, which probably pissed off Hugh even more. Even his own goddamn brother was giving money away to rival firms, like a Ford dealer driving a Chevy. But Hugh's reluctance to move the stuff and his turning down deals to distribute for Cantrell throughout Iowa had left the door open for Cantrell to move in. Hugh would never admit that, though.

"So as you know," Hugh began. "This mess with Cantrell is a thorn in our side."

"One step closer to being put to rest after tonight though, right?" Calvin asked.

"We hope." Hugh and Victor shared a look that did not instill confidence in Calvin.

"Thing is," Victor said. "We've been getting intel from inside the Cantrell camp." He smiled with long white teeth. "We've got a spy."

"You've got one means he's got one," Calvin said. He didn't believe in blowing smoke. He was a realist. People who talked just to make themselves feel better were more likely to get caught with their pants down.

"Maybe," Hugh said. "But we've learned a few things and one of them concerns you."

"Me? How the fuck does Cantrell even know who I am?"

"You see there's this list..."

"A hit list," Vic clarified.

Calvin wanted that beer now. "And I'm on it?"

"Afraid so." Hugh ashtrayed his cigar and stood. "A lot of people are, including me and Victor."

"Even our dad," Victor said.

"How the hell did I get dragged into this?"

"We figure it was those guys you let go on the highway. They must have gone back to Cantrell and put in a description of you. You're kind of a legend in these parts, y'know?"

Calvin drew a hand across the bristles of his high and tight. "Heartless bastards. I let them live and this is how they repay me?"

Hugh poured himself a bourbon. "We thought you should know."

"Great. Now I know, what the hell do I do about it?"

"We've got contacts we've checked with to see if the contract has been taken up by anyone. There's a broker who works out of the quad cities. Handles some of the top guys." Hugh and Victor nodded along with each other at the memory. "We had his guy Quarry take care of a problem for us once. Did a top job. But this broker says nobody on his payroll has the contract."

"You think he'd tell you if they did?"

"We're taking precautions, Cal." Hugh took a firm tone, trying to put an end to the discussion.

"Like what? Do I get a bodyguard?"

Hugh lowered his chin, looked at Cal from under his brow. "Precautions."

Victor chimed in with that high energy combination of

the last coke in his system and his body starting to crave more. "Besides, after tonight I bet he's running scared back to Nebraska to fuck a pig or whatever those hayseeds do over there."

You'd think Iowa was the Holy Land the way Vic talked shit about every other state. Don't get him started on Minnesota.

"Well, shit. I really kinda want to get home and check on Dorothy now."

"You go, Cal. We'll check in later. You let us know if anything seems fishy, okay?"

"Hugh, by the time I figure out something is fishy I'll have two slugs in my chest or a rope around my neck."

Hugh put out his hand to shake. "Thanks again for tonight. And for everything."

Calvin took his hand. "Guess I'm in it up to my eyeballs now."

"Some kind of balls, anyway," Vic said.

Hugh didn't smile at the joke. He eyed Calvin squarely. "Welcome to our side of the fence."

Victor closed the door behind Calvin as he left. The brothers were shutting themselves in to talk more about these precautions.

Calvin felt a hand on his arm and he was pulled off balance. He nearly struck out with a balled up fist until he noticed it was Nancy tugging him along down the hall. She pushed him into a small laundry room and kicked the door closed with her foot. She wore a black negligee over Italian lingerie and garter belts.

"Calvin McGraw, you're going to fuck me now."

"Nancy, not now."

She stomped her foot, put on a pout like a grade school girl. "You know how many of these guys I've fucked? It's not like you're violating the sanctity of a marriage here."

"You only want this because I'm the only one who says no."

"You're damn right."

"Well, here it is again. No. Now let me get the hell out of here, I got bigger things on my mind."

"I swear to God, Calvin, if you don't put me out of my misery—"

"What? Huh? Let me tell you something, Nancy, there is precious little you could do right now that is worse than the situation I'm already in."

He watched her change tactics. She softened, ran a gentle hand across his chest in the narrow confines of the laundry room.

"There's a way to alleviate your guilt, you know?"

Calvin grabbed her wrists and held them off his body. "I don't have time for this."

"Get rid of Victor," she whispered. "If he goes away, so do all our troubles."

"All *your* troubles, Nancy. And even that's bullshit. I love my wife. It's not your husband who's keeping me away from you. Hell, it's not even my wife. It's you. This desperate act might work on the young studs around here but it just makes me sad for you. And it's getting annoying. So get the hell out of my way 'cause I got bigger fish to fry."

He turned her body and backed away from her to the door. Nancy's face burned with anger. He thought she might scream or claw at his face with her brightly painted nails, but she stood there and simmered until he shut the door.

12

Dorothy met Calvin at the door with a cold beer, top already cracked and still foaming.

"Well, you were gone a long time," she said.

"Don't I know it." He took a sip of his beer and exhaled into his favorite chair. He thought about putting on the TV, maybe trying for the last half hour of Johnny Carson, but he was too tired.

Dorothy followed him into the living room, took her seat in the chair opposite his—hers in little yellow flowers, his in tan corduroy. "So what happened?"

He didn't want to frighten her. This news about the hit list would amount to nothing, he knew. No reason to stir up Dorothy over it.

"Just a drop and wait job. Delivering the boys to a job and then bringing them back home."

She watched him like a lawyer and he was on the stand. She noticed when he wouldn't meet her eyes, staring down into his beer can like he'd dropped something there. Dorothy knew Calvin McGraw was a capable liar, but not to her.

"So why do you look so worried?"

He caught her eye for second, had to turn away from the

intense heat there. He knew from experience he wouldn't be able to stall her. As his bullshit got deeper, the more missteps he took until finally his boots were full of the stuff and she'd got all out of him she wanted to get.

They told each other near everything and he decided his best choice was to substitute a truth she could handle for a truth he didn't want to tell.

"It's Nancy, Vic's wife."

Dorothy arched an eyebrow. "Oh, really?"

"Now listen, there's no funny business going on, but she's after me like a bloodhound after a polecat. Just talk, though. I won't let her get close enough to me to light my cigarette."

"You don't smoke."

"Well, if I did." Calvin knew he sounded a bit flustered. It might work to his advantage here. Distract Dorothy with the truth about Nancy and she might be satisfied.

"So she's after you, huh?"

"Like white on rice. She wants to be, anyways."

"Why you?"

Calvin gave her a furrowed brow look. "Now what the hell is that supposed to mean? I'm good enough for you, ain't I?"

"You know what I mean."

"I'm afraid I don't. If it's so mysterious why a woman could have the hots for me then I think the first person you ought to ask why to is the woman in the mirror."

"Okay, Cal. What's she doing?"

"Propositioning me, that's what."

"Like what? What does she say?"

Calvin set down his beer can on the side table, missing the coaster there. "Dot, you don't want to get into all that crap. I shot her down like a mallard duck on the opening day of the season. She won't come around no more. It's just got me in a spin is all. Nobody wants another man's wife putting the hit on him."

He wondered if his words were too close to the other truth bubbling below the surface.

"I think a lot of men would like that, actually," Dorothy said.

"Well, not this one."

"Maybe you should. Might get you fired, then you wouldn't have to quit."

"You're lucky I know you're joking. A lot of men would love a free pass at a woman like that."

"A woman like that, huh?"

"You know what I mean."

Dorothy smiled. "I guess I do."

"I'm just keeping you in the loop is all."

Dorothy stood up, patted the back of his hand. "I know you, old coot."

"I'm hardly old."

She lifted his beer can and set it on the coaster with the varnished photo of Door County, Wisconsin they got on a summer trip six years ago. A young couple waterskiing. Dot brushed the hair above his ears.

"I see some grey."

"I don't think that's an area you want to go comparing."

"You forget, Calvin McGraw, I know you well enough to know when you know it's a good idea to lie to me." She kissed his forehead. "I'm going to bed now. Don't stay up too late."

Did she know there was more he wasn't telling her? After all these years together the woman had become a damn Gypsy with her ways to seeing into his head.

"Oh, Cal," she said, turning in the doorway to the stairs. "Have you heard from Webb? Seems like he ought to be back by now."

Goddamn, it did. Calvin had been caught up in his own mess of shit he hadn't thought about his son out there on the road trying to deliver his first solo job. He had a lot of miles to put under his belt, but if he drove straight through he should be back. The Mercury wasn't prone to breakdowns, certainly nothing Webb couldn't fix quick. And if they're'd been any trouble with the pick-up, Calvin certainly hadn't heard about it.

"Oh, he's alright. Had to go pretty far down south. He'll probably be back by morning."

Dorothy smiled with tight lips and turned for the stairs. Calvin sat in his chair and finished his beer thinking to himself how his wife could see through him like a wisp of smoke.

Had Webb been too young for a solo job? No way. Cal trained him up himself. The boy was solid. But if the kid wasn't home by morning, his week just got a whole lot worse right about when he thought that was no longer an option.

***

Webb didn't want to stop in a motel. They were only ten miles from the Iowa/Missouri border when he gave in to Joni's nagging and pulled over to a place with a neon sign advertising COMFORTABLE BEDS, HOURLY RATES and AIR CONDITIONING.

"You dragged your feet all day and don't think I didn't notice," he told her.

The smug look on her face said back, *yeah, but you let me.*

"Is this the Indy Five Hundred or something? What's the

rush to get back to fucking Iowa?"

"It's my job."

"So you want to bring me back at eleven at night, unshowered, wake up Mr. Stanley and dump me on his doorstep? Is that how you want this to go?"

Webb had no response. Delivering her so late at night would look bad. His instructions were to deliver her directly to Hugh Stanley, no middlemen. So it was a midnight knock on his door or nothing. Chances were good he'd be awake, but what if he wasn't? And when was a midnight visit a good thing?

Webb had to weigh the difference between waiting another day to deliver the girl, or dropping in so late at night he looked like an amateur? Which was worse?

"Plus," she said, "this is the last night of my freedom. Until I get old or fat, I guess. You're gonna deny a girl her last chance to live it up?"

While the decision spun in his head, he looked up and saw the sign ahead, so he pulled off.

"Stop at the gas station and get us some beer or something."

"I'm not doing that," he said.

"Come on, Webb. It's my last night. Would you deny one of your buddies on his last night before he got drafted?"

"This is hardly the same thing."

"Bullshit. I'm going off to some place I don't want to go to suffer indignities all being decided upon by men in dark suits who have no idea what it's like for the grunts down below getting fucked at every turn."

"Spare me the hippie bullshit."

"It's not hippie bullshit, it's the truth. You know how many Americans have died in Vietnam? Too many."

"You got a real mouth on you, you know that?"

"Yeah, and I use it to say real shit. It's not just for breathing and blowing."

Joni turned in her seat, crossed her arms over her chest and pouted. Without admitting defeat, he gave in to her again for at least the tenth time that day and pulled into a Shell station next to the motel. He gave her five bucks and she went inside to buy a six pack while he stayed outside to fill up the Mercury. He watched her through the glass walls of the gas station market. She'd thrown off her pout and practically skipped to the beer cooler. She brought the six pack to the front and gave shy girl eyes to the man behind the counter. Webb watched as he flushed red from something she said. She sure as hell knew how to lay it on thick when she wanted to. With her silver tongue Webb didn't doubt she figured a way to talk the clerk into giving her the six for free.

She threw her bag down on one of the twin beds in the exhausted looking room.

"Not my first choice for where to spend my last night before I go into lockup, but beggars can't be choosers, right?" She cracked the top on a beer, her second. The first she'd finished in the car before Webb had even found a parking space.

"You make it sound like you're going to prison."

"Aren't I?" She locked eyes with Webb as she took another long gulp of beer. The stare made him uncomfortable. He excused himself to the bathroom and let go a long piss. He heard her outside singing *Cecilia* by Simon & Garfunkel, but she clearly only knew the words to the chorus.

When he came back into the room she was on her third

beer.

"So did you run away or something?" Webb asked. He figured it might be his last chance to know. As soon as the question left his mouth he knew he'd stepped over a line. His dad would be disappointed.

"Something," she said.

"You don't have to tell me."

"No. It's okay." She finished beer number three. He tossed her number four. "Thanks. I was working in one of the Stanley's clubs. Slinging drinks, dancing on weeknights. Y'know how it goes. Girl like me with a high school diploma but all anyone wants to look at are my tits."

Webb whipped his eyes to the carpet, afraid he'd been looking at her chest without realizing it.

"Not a whole lot of options for a girl like me. Mr. Stanley comes in and takes a shine to me. What am I gonna do? He pays my check, right? And it's always good to get in nice with the boss. So I let him have a tumble. Guess I did it too good though because next I know I'm being invited to his house for private parties. Ten or eleven guys, a dozen or so girls. It always ended up with me and him in his bed at the end of the night."

Webb debated reaching for one of the beers, but he sat still on the edge of his twin bed, listening to her story.

"Pretty soon he's talking about me leaving the club and moving in with him. I'd seen other girls there. He's like Hugh Hefner, y'know?" Her eyes lit up. "Hey, they even have the same name. Huh. I just realized that. Crazy, right?"

"Crazy," Webb said.

"So anyways, I'd seen other girls around and I knew all I was doing was replacing one. Some girl was gonna get booted to the street because of me. And all I'd ever do was hang around at his place. Where's the fun in that? So I bailed. I mean, last I checked, it's a free country, right?"

"So they say."

"Exactly." She drained her fourth beer, let loose a belch that would make a truck driver proud, and collapsed back on the bed with a laugh. "Why do they call these damn things twin beds? You can't fit two people on here."

Webb watched her loose shirt open to show most of one breast. He saw her flat belly pushed out from the beer. Her legs were lean and looked like dancers legs. Her hair was the color of a girl in a shampoo ad.

She turned her head to him. "What do you think? Could we fit two people in this bed?"

Something about the way she looked through him, straight into his eyes and out the other side, made him read deeper into her question. She hadn't said it trying to be sultry, hadn't given a wink or pushed out her chest. But he knew what she meant and blood rushed from his head as it sank in.

"Webb? Could we?"

"I bet we could," he said. "But we shouldn't."

"Why not."

"My job. You know."

She pushed up and leaned on her elbows, her hair falling over her face, her lips wet from the beer. "But what if I want to know what it feels like to have someone my own age touch me before I have to..." She lowered her eyes.

Webb felt genuine guilt. He knew what he'd be delivering this girl to in the morning. He understood why she ran away. He knew she could never forgive him for taking her back.

He'd bought her clothes. Bought her beer. Let her stay on

the outside for another night. What's one more gift to a girl before she steps behind those prison walls?

Webb pushed off his bed and leaned over on to hers. Their bodies barely fit. He had to lean over her, his face close enough to hers he could smell the beer.

13

Calvin had to wait an hour and change before anyone named Stanley showed up to the office. Not exactly a regular hours kind of crowd. Coffee was cold, the sun high overhead and his foot had fallen asleep from sitting cross-legged in the waiting room chairs.

He wanted Hugh, but got Vic.

"McGraw. Good, I need to talk to you," Vic said as he passed him on his way into his office. Mirrored shades sat on his head. His wide-lapeled shirt hung open to his sternum and a thick gold chain tangled in his chest hair.

Calvin stood up and followed him in. "I need to talk to you too."

Vic ran a finger over a small mirror on his desk, then he rubbed the finger on his gums. "I think I know what this is about." He flopped into his chair. Motioned for Calvin to do the same.

"Have a seat. You go first." He held up a finger, pausing Calvin before he could start. He raised his voice, "Cheryl, some fuckin' coffee in here."

Vic gestured for Calvin to continue. The floor to ceiling windows behind him backlit Vic with a washed out yellow glow. The glass radiated heat into the room and Calvin felt like he would start sweating at any moment. He swallowed and said what he came there for.

"I wanna know what's being done for my protection."

Vic sat up straighter in his chair. Clearly this wasn't what he expected. "What's that mean?"

"You tell me last night that there's a hit out on me. I want to know what's being done about it."

"We told you we're taking care of it."

"Yeah, but how?"

"Look, McGraw, there's way more Stanleys on that list than there are of you. We're working on it is all I can say. If you're scared and afraid you're gonna piss your panties, go take a vacation or some shit."

Calvin's leg bounced with excess energy. "It's my family," he said. "Are they at risk?"

"You know as much as we know right now, okay? Probably it's all bullshit and Cantrell doesn't have the balls to fill his own sack, let alone carry out a hit on us. And I hate to say it, McGraw, but your name was pretty far down the list. If they're coming heavy, we'll know it before they get to you."

"Or maybe they'll start with the easy targets," he said. "That's what I'd do."

Vic scratched at his unshaven chin. "Cheryl, the fuckin' coffee." Calvin knew he wanted to swirl some powder in his brew, but with company in the room with him he could still fake that his secret was safe.

Calvin decided to dip a toe in the water. "This is the kind of shit that makes me think about hanging my hat and getting out." He watched Vic for a reaction, but Victor waved him off, not even considering that a McGraw would quit.

"Look, McGraw, we got other issues."

Cheryl entered with a fresh pot of coffee and two mugs. She set the tray down and poured one for Victor, let the other mug remain empty.

"Thanks, doll," Vic said. Then to Calvin, "Help yourself."

Calvin let the mug sit. Vic sipped and smacked his lips at the heat. "Damn."

"What other issues?" Calvin asked.

Vic tipped open a small box on his desk, lifted a letter opener and dipped it inside, bringing out a small mound of powder. "Sugar," he said, then swirled the white into the mug. He didn't seem to care if Calvin knew or not.

Calvin stayed sitting forward, not relaxed, far from at ease.

"What other issues, Vic?"

Vic muscled down a slug of the hot coffee. "One big one," he said. "Are you banging my wife?"

Calvin's face fell for a second and then a flush of anger took over. His cheeks got hot and his hands balled into fists.

"No."

"But she asked you to, right?"

Cal didn't know what Vic knew or what lies Nancy had fed him. His best defense was the truth. No need to protect her.

"She has, yes."

"I freakin' knew it." Vic slurped more coffee, wiping at his scalded lips. "She's fuckin' a bunch of these guys. I know she is."

He waved his finger around as if the room was filled with his bodyguards and muscle men. Calvin stayed quiet, unsure where this could be headed.

"Will you do me a favor, McGraw? Do me a kindness?"

"What's that?"

"Let her."

Calvin stared. "Let her what?"

"Let her fuck you. Or at least make her think she's gonna."

"I'm not gonna do that."

"You gotta."

"What the hell for?"

The caffeine and cocaine had hit his system. His eyes pulled a little wider, hands shook a little more. "So I can get rid of her."

Calvin really wished he'd gotten Hugh instead. "Kill her? Are you crazy?"

"Relax, McGraw. I want to catch her in the act and take photos." Vic leaned forward, elbows on his desk. A salesman. "I ask for a divorce and she gets half my shit, right? I go to a lawyer with pictures of her doing some other guy and she goes away quietly. Oh, who am I kidding, she'll scream and shout, but I can give her the boot back to her parents or some shit. I really don't give a crap where she goes as long as it's gone."

"Not me. Ask one of the others."

"They're the hired help, McGraw. I need someone I can trust. I need someone she can't buy off or offer to suck and fuck until he rolls over on me in court."

Calvin never expected his loyalty and dedication would lead to this.

"Can't you go see a counselor or something? Work it out?"

"It's too late, McGraw. You can see that." Vic came around and sat on the edge of his desk, facing Calvin. "Now you'll do this thing for me."

"I really don't feel comfortable with it."

"I don't think I was asking."

Calvin got it. Do this for him or suffer the consequences, whatever those were. Thing was with consequences, none of them were good. Calvin tried to buy him off with a delay, "I'll think about it."

"You know her, McGraw. I don't get rid of her one way or another and she'll be the goddamn death of me."

Calvin wasn't going to argue that. He stood and left the office while he could, thinking— *yeah, I really need to get away from this nutball family.*

14

A Peterbilt outside started up with the sound of a boulder rolling down a hill. Webb jerked awake and felt the stale humidity of the room over him like a film. The heat and sweat from the night before with Joni was trapped in the cheap motel room and it brought vivid memories back to him right away. He wasn't sure if she would have such a clear vision of their night together after she'd polished off the entire six pack, but Webb was glad he'd kept his head clear.

The truck roared away and Webb cracked through sleep crusted eyes to look at the curtains, a sick yellow/orange, as they fought to keep out the sun slanting in. He turned to find an empty pillow beside him. He looked up to the bathroom door. It hung open, a fly buzzing in and out of the tiny room, undecided where to land.

He pushed himself up on his elbows, scanned the room left to right. No Joni. Six empty beer cans crowded the tiny plastic trash can, the empty wrapper off a courtesy glass sat crumpled on the nightstand. No other signs of her. No bag, no shoes, no note saying when she'd return. Only the lingering scent of their sex as her goodbye.

He sat up, noticed he was still naked, and covered himself

with the thin sheet from the bed. She could be out getting more beer. Hair of the dog. He panicked. Found his jeans and dug through the pockets. The keys to the Eliminator were still there. She didn't take the car but the minimart was walking distance away.

Webb pulled on his pants and left quickly, leaving the door unlocked.

He stalked around the outside of the gas station market, peering in the windows like a visitor at the zoo. No Joni. He went inside, realizing only as he passed the sign that he wasn't wearing shoes. If they refused him service, fine. He just had a question.

"You see a girl in here? Blonde. Pretty. White macrame handbag?"

The clerk was a skinny guy with a three dimensional Adam's apple. "When?"

"This morning. Probably not long ago."

"Nope."

"Shit."

Webb pounded out the door trying to go over in his head how bad this was. Hugh would be pissed. His dad would be pissed, maybe more.

"Shit, shit, shit."

A mother guided her son in a wide arc around Webb as they headed for the restroom. He realized what he must look like, no shoes and sleep-tussled hair shouting obscenities at no one. He went back to the motel.

She still wasn't there.

Calvin walked past Cheryl who held the phone to her ear with an attachment that set a crescent moon shape on her shoulder and let her talk hands free, keeping her open for nail polishing, magazine reading or nose picking. The wonders of the space age.

"Oh, Calvin," she said. "Your son on the phone for you."

Cal took a second to process. "Webb? For me?"

"Yeah. He sounds kinda out of breath or something."

Calvin spotted a phone extension in the corner by a potted plant. "Can you put it through over there?"

"Sure thing." Cheryl pressed two buttons and the extension rang.

"Webb, where the hell are you? Your mom is worried sick."

"I just talked to her. She told me you were there."

"That trip shouldn't have taken you so long, son."

"Dad, listen to me. She's gone."

Calvin sat down and dropped his voice, turning his head toward the plant. "The cargo?"

"Yeah, Dad. She split."

He spit out his angriest whisper. "How the fuck did that happen?"

"We were in a motel for the night. When I woke up she was gone."

"Because you should have been back yesterday. Why the fuck were you in a motel?"

Webb didn't want to get into it. "Dad, what do I do?"

"You find her, that's what."

Webb flopped back on the bed, the sheets still in a tangle from last night. He pressed his eyelids until he saw stars.

"How bad is it?"

Calvin let a long pause go by which didn't make Webb feel any better.

"It ain't good."

"Jesus, Dad, I fucked up. I fucked up as bad as I could. I'm so sorry."

"It ain't me you gotta apologize to and it ain't me you gotta be worried about. It's the Stanleys."

Webb knew it, but hearing it hurt like a hornet sting. He rapped a fist against his forehead, trying to knock an idea loose in his brain. "Someone had to have seen her, right?"

"Someone did. You just gotta find 'em."

"Okay. Okay. I'll go look for her."

"You do that," Calvin said. "And son?" Another long break. Webb waited for it like a man in the gallows listening for the snap of rope. "You find her or you don't come back, you hear?"

"I hear you, Dad."

Calvin hung up and sat still for a moment. This talk of getting out had been too late. He sat and thought what the hell he'd done to his son. What the hell he was going to do about Vic's proposition. What the hell he was going to do about the death threat against him.

This was why the goddamn car was invented. To get up and get out. If Henry Ford was sitting next to him on the shit brown sofa, he'd say, "Calvin, get behind that wheel and go. Drive anywhere. This country's got a hundred thousand miles of open road, all of it yours. Men died cutting highway through mountain passes. There are roads straight as the edge of a razor and crooked as a politician. Go on out there and grab hold of one and don't let go."

But damn if he wasn't sitting on four flat tires.

Webb dressed and patted the keys in his front pocket. He went to the front desk of the motel.

"Did you see the girl I was with?"

The chubby man behind the counter looked up from a comic book through dirty glasses. A fly buzzed away from a scab at his lip. "Girl?"

"Yeah, the one I came in with last night. Real pretty. Blonde."

"Oh, yeah," he said, shifting a wad of chewing gum from one side of his mouth to tuck in the cheek of the other. "She came by this morning."

"She say where she was going?"

Chubby smiled with yellow nubs for teeth. "She run out on you?"

"Did she say where she was off to?"

"I figured you wasn't married."

Webb slammed his hand down on the counter with a crack like lightning.

"She asked me which way to the highway and maybe some place to get a bite to eat. I thought she was just a working girl moving on after a trick."

Webb thought she kind of was. "What way did you send her?"

"To Arlo's, by the exit ramp." He pointed a fat finger south. "Can't be more than a mile."

"What time?"

Chubby thought for a second. "Couldn't have been much more than two hours."

Shit. Two hours was a decent lead. Joni could be long gone and Webb would be on the run. Well, if he was going to run, he might as well be chasing something at the same time.

15

Two steps in the door and—"Did Webb get ahold of you?"
Calvin kept walking to the kitchen. "Yeah, I talked to him."

Dorothy followed him. "I'm glad he's all right. What did he
want to talk to you about? It sounded urgent."

Calvin pulled open the fridge, dug inside for a beer. "Car
trouble. He got stuck in Missouri with a bad alternator."
Talking to the back of the fridge and without meeting
Dorothy's eyes made the lie easier. He straightened out of the
refrigerator with his beer.

"I'm not so sure I like all the lies around here lately."

"Lies? What lies?" Inside he said, *oh shit*.

"Calvin McGraw, it's ten thirty in the morning and you're
drinking a beer. Either I need to get you over to the church
basement for a meeting, or you've got something on your
mind."

The plus from this whole Nancy situation was the easy
excuse of something legit that was troubling his brain and
causing him a knife point of pain in his stomach.

"You won't believe what Vic said to me today." He cracked
the tab on his Pabst Blue Ribbon.

Dorothy crossed her arms. "What now?"

Calvin took a sip of beer. "Wants me to help him set up Nancy. Make it look like we're screwing so he can snap pictures and keep her from dragging out a divorce."

She read truth in his words. And better than that, this was good gossip. Dorothy was shy of friends and those she had she couldn't hardly talk to about Calvin's work. Good old fashioned tales out of school were hard to come by in her book club at the library. When Heather slept with the bag boy at the Hy-Vee last spring it was fodder enough for six months of chatter among the ladies. Since then the well had run dry.

"What happened?"

"He knows she's fooling around. Wants to trap her and keep her from bleeding him dry in a settlement."

"What did you say?"

"I said no, of course." He held his arms out wide, asking *what do you take me for?*

Dorothy leaned against the counter top. "So what's going to happen?"

"I don't know. Vic's gotten out of control. Too much of the ol booger sugar." Calvin tapped the side of his nose.

Dorothy leaned in closer. This story kept getting better. "Really?"

"Yeah. That's been going on a while now. I figure Hugh has to know, but maybe something needs to be done about it."

"You really think you can get them to turn on each other?"

"No." He took another sip. "I'd no sooner drive a wedge between the Stanley boys than climb Mount Everest in my Sunday best. But I gotta do something." He set his beer down and ran a tired hand down over his face. "I gotta do something."

Dorothy saw the strain on him. Even if she was unaware

101

of the full load he carried, she knew his trouble weighed a ton. She stepped over and put her arms around him. They embraced each other, each holding on tight. Calvin wished they were on open highway, wind through the window, horizon fading away to nothing. His feet never felt so cemented to one place before in his life.

Trapped by circumstance and nothing to do but stay and fight it out.

***

The front tires of the Mercury banged over the edge of the curb as Webb pulled into the parking lot of Arlo's, a greasy spoon catering to the highway crowd. There were a handful of cars including a station wagon with a roof rack piled high with suitcases and a pickup truck smeared with mud.

Web steadied himself before getting out, deciding that a less panicked approach would yield more results. A man desperate to find a girl might have another agenda for her when he catches up.

Inside he went straight to the counter and found a waitress with a hairdo that nearly scraped the ceiling fans.

"Hi, sugar," she said. "Sit anywhere you like."

"I'm actually looking for a girl I think might have come in here. Blonde and pretty, name's Joni? She's my kid sister and we missed each other where we were supposed to meet. She always was lousy with directions." Webb forced a smile he hoped didn't look too needy.

"Oh, yeah, I seen her this morning. 'Bout an hour ago. I didn't get her name but that sure sounds like her."

Webb looked around the restaurant hoping to see her

lurking in a booth. "That's great. Is she still around?"

"I don't think so." The waitress turned and shouted back to the kitchen. "Hey, Arlo."

A man of enormous girth appeared in the door, a stack of receipts in one hand and a sandwich thick as a phonebook in the other. "Yeah?"

"You remember that girl you talked to this morning? Pretty l'il thing? This here's her brother and he's looking for her."

"She moved on," Arlo said and he began to turn back to his business.

Webb leaned over the counter. "Did she say where she was going?"

Arlo stopped. "She hitched a ride with Big Dan which I told her wasn't the smartest move, but she seemed awful headstrong if you ask me."

Definitely the right girl, Webb thought. "Who's Big Dan?"

The waitress took over and let Arlo lumber back to his office.

"He's a trucker. Stops by here on his run. Mobile to Omaha and back once a week. Been coming in here for near ten years."

"Which way was he headed? To Omaha or to Mobile?"

"On his way back down south. You sure your sister knew she was supposed to meet you?"

Webb's shoulders sunk. "He's right. She is headstrong. A little stupid sometimes." He tapped a finger on the counter, ignoring the stares of an older fella half way down the counter. Probably the guy with the muddy truck. "About an hour ago you said?"

"I think so. I try not to watch the clock too much, sugar. You know what they say about a watched pot. I start watching those arms sweep around and they slow down and my shift never seems to end."

"Thanks for your help. Better give me a tall cup of coffee to go."

She moved on down the counter to get it for him. Webb figured when they left, Big Dan would have been fueled up and well fed. They wouldn't need to stop for a while so he could keep on down the road for a few hours before he needed to start pulling off at every truck stop and highway diner he found. The path to Mobile would take them past St. Louis if he was willing to make a slight detour so Webb had to assume Joni was headed back where he picked her up. It was a start anyway.

All he could think was he should have seen it coming.

16

Calvin hadn't gone back for a second beer. Day drinking wasn't going to solve his problems. He sat listening to George Jones on the Hi-Fi taking some small comfort in the knowledge that at least someone else had problems causing him worry. Maybe George's troubles weren't as a life threatening, but Ol' George sure had about as many problems weighing him down as Calvin did right then.

Getting out was still an option, but they couldn't leave without Webb. And if Calvin up and bailed in the middle of a crisis like this war with Cantrell's clan, he'd been seen as yellow and a traitor. Worse, they might think he was a mole working for the other side. Someone sure as hell was feeding Cantrell info.

When the phone rang he didn't want to pick it up. Something about the ring sounded off. Same ring as always, but there was a sixth sense he had that it brought bad news.

Six rings in and he lifted the receiver.

"Gas her up, McGraw," Hugh Stanley said.

"What now?"

"We got word that Cantrell is making a move. It's the list, Cal. And he's starting at the top. I need you to go get

Edmond."

Edmond Stanley, the patriarch of the family. An old fashioned prohibition era rumrunner and a pioneer in Iowa crime history. Now, though, the Stanley sons kept him shut away in their childhood home on a hill overlooking the river. They didn't consult him, they didn't ask advice. They spent most of their time denying he's still alive. Edmond always looked about two steps from the grave, but somehow he kept chugging along like an engine that wouldn't die despite all the miles on it. "They're after Edmond?"

"It's symbolic," Hugh said. "But we won't give them the satisfaction. I want you to get him and bring him here. He'll be safe. We're circling the wagons, Cal. We need you."

Calvin still recalled meeting the old man when he was coming up on the heels of his own pops. Edmond always gave him a tussle of his mop of straw-colored hair and usually had a lollipop or a stick of gum in his pocket to share. Edmond was one of the only men Calvin could recall from back then who didn't smoke. Always kept his pockets full of sweets and when the others would light up, he'd throw in a sucker and the thin stick would match everyone else's tobacco rolls.

For history, for respect, Calvin didn't hesitate.

"I'll go."

"Thanks, Cal. And don't worry. Right now Cantrell and his crew are a line of ants marching, but we're a big black boot coming down."

Hugh hung up and Calvin went to get his keys.

"Was that Webb?" Dorothy asked.

"No, it was Hugh. I have to go out and collect up the old man on the hill."

"Edmond? Why?"

106

"I don't ask why. I just drive."

He saw the spark of skepticism in her eye. It's hard to keep someone in the dark when they give off so much light.

"Back soon," he said and kissed her lightly on the cheek. He paused at the door, thought about the list and how far down Cantrell might go. Hugh seemed insistent on reassuring him he would be safe, but then Hugh would say anything to get his agenda dealt with first. He was the boss, and don't you forget it. "Be on the lookout, okay?"

"The lookout for what?" Dorothy's voice grew even more suspicious.

Calvin pulled a fast one out of thin air. "For Webb. If he got the car going again he should be back any time now."

He left his flimsy lie behind and walked out. Like a band aid on a bullet hole, it had to do for now.

If he was honest, Calvin liked being back in a car. He went to the garage and selected the Buick Gran Sport GSX for this job. It was his newest car and he'd been ignoring it, but no more. He always heard a lot of guys talk about a favorite chair at home they liked to watch TV in or just sit and have a drink. His favorite chair was a driver's seat. Maybe it was the movement, the forward momentum. It felt like doing something. You were going somewhere. Making something happen. Not sitting idly by and waiting for the world.

He controlled how fast he went, what turns he took. It made him think how much being in the front office of a racing company would suck and possibly bore him into a rope around his neck.

He steered the Buick onto the street where Edmond's house balanced on the top of a small crest. The house was a battleship gray with a high peaked roof and two dormer windows that looked like eyes and made the house seem like it was suspicious of you. It looked gothic and probably scared the neighborhood kids, especially since an old man lived there who never went out.

Coming the opposite way down the street was a four door sedan. It took a sharp angle across the road and stopped with a jerk at the curb out front of Edmond's. Three men got out and made for the house. One man stayed behind.

Shit. Calvin was moments too late.

The new car didn't have a gun stashed in the glove box and Edmond didn't have security the way Hugh and Vic did. The two ungrateful sons didn't want to pay somebody to watch over the old man they worked so hard to ignore.

Calvin wasn't sure exactly what he would do, but he wasn't going to let Edmond be carried away without a fight.

He parked four doors down from Edmond's and behind the sedan. He got out, went to the trunk and withdrew the tire iron. He walked slowly toward the sedan, keeping an eye on the rearview mirror he could see through the back window. The driver's eyes never glanced up. Dumb. Dumber still, he'd turned off the engine. So much for a quick getaway. And his hands were off the wheel while he smoked.

Amateur.

The window was rolled down and Calvin waited for the man to ash out onto the sidewalk before he walked up and put the tip of the tire iron to the back of the driver's neck. He couldn't see it wasn't a gun, only felt cold steel and heard someone say, "Hands up and don't move."

The driver lifted his hands and Calvin watched every muscle in his body tense. He wore a cowboy hat with deep bends in the brim, a thick mustache and hair grown down past his ears. One of them hippie types Calvin hated so much.

"Keys," Calvin said. He watched as the man slowly reached forward and took the key out of the ignition. He could see a holster on the man's hip. "And the gun."

The driver handed the keys and a .38 snubnose out the window to Calvin who let the tire iron clang to the sidewalk once he had the real gun pressed against the driver's head, lifting the hat up off his head a few inches.

"What's your name?"

"Richie."

"Okay, Richie. You go on and get inside the trunk for me."

"What—" He had to stop and swallow. "What are you gonna do?"

"We're talking about what *you're* going to do right now, Richie. And you're going to get in the trunk."

Calvin opened the door and stepped back while Richie tried to climb out with his hands still held high. His cigarette dropped ash down his shirt collar. "Oh, fuck."

Calvin thrust the gun forward. "No sudden moves."

Richie went still, then inched forward like he was trapped in quickly hardening cement.

"You can go faster than that," Calvin said.

He got Richie back to the trunk and watched him climb in. The cowboy hat fell off and Calvin had an idea. He picked it up and kept it, then slammed the trunk as Richie tried to plead for his life.

Ideas came quick and before he could second guess himself, Calvin went with it. He opened the trunk again, sure to have the gun out and ready in case Richie got any ideas.

"Give me your shirt," he said.

"What the fuck for?" Richie asked.

Calvin aimed the gun between Richie's eyes and repeated his command. "Give me your shirt."

"Jesus, okay, okay." Richie struggled in the trunk like a fat baby in a crib but managed to get his shirt off and hand it to Calvin who slammed the trunk lid closed again before Richie was ready. He felt the metal bang off the top of Richie's head.

Calvin wrapped the gun in the shirt, leaned the cowboy hat against the front tire of the sedan, then went to the driver's side, leaned in and pressed the horn three times for one second each. Something that couldn't be confused with normal traffic sounds. They may have already had a signal like shave and haircut or a Morse code SOS, but Calvin doubted they thought that far ahead. On the third horn blast he fired a shot into the tire and through the cowboy hat.

He unwrapped the gun and tossed the shirt aside, picked up the hat and its still-smoldering bullet hole and ducked next to a tall bush to wait and see what his lure caught.

A few seconds later one of the men came down the steps. Another long hair, he wore a tight T-shirt, flared jeans with a woven rope belt. He carried another snubnose in his hand. He came around to the car looking for Richie.

"Richie?" He stepped in front of the bush with his back to Calvin.

Calvin placed the gun to the new man's temple and said, "Drop it."

The hippie's hands went up, his knees shook. Rank amateurs, all of them.

"I said drop it."

The hippie did. Calvin pulled one of his arms down and bent it like a chicken wing behind his back. The hippie grunted but didn't cry out. Calvin thought about honking the horn again and maybe having luck enough to lure them out one by one, but he doubted it would work twice, let alone three times. Plus he'd have to keep stuffing more and more of them in the trunk. And in all that time, Edmond could be dead inside. He needed to get in there.

"Are you here to kill the old man?" Calvin asked.

"It's a snatch job."

"Take him back to Cantrell?"

When the hippie didn't answer, Calvin wrenched his arm up higher until he gave out a, "Yeah."

"What's taking them so long, then?"

"Getting some information out of him."

Calvin worried. "He doesn't know shit."

"He ain't saying shit."

Calvin knew what getting information entailed. Edmond wouldn't live through much torture. Calvin knew he had to go in. He shoved the hippie forward.

"You give up info real easy yourself there, pal."

"You were gonna shoot me," the hippie said.

Calvin had no intention to shoot him, not if he could help it. These punks might be sadistic enough to blast someone as soon as look at them, but Calvin wanted to keep his relatively clean record intact. As he took the steps behind his prisoner, he doubted he could pull it off.

He heard voices from the kitchen. A slap like an open palm on raw meat. He shoved the hippie forward, using the body to block his own, the gun at his head. "Go," he said.

They stopped in the doorway.

"Drop 'em," Calvin said.

The two men looked up and saw their partner filling the

111

doorway. Calvin's body was almost completely hidden behind the hippie and the door frame. He could see Edmond sitting in a chrome legged chair, a line of blood drooling from his nose. Dark patches in his four day growth of stubble. Cal hadn't seen the senior Stanley in years. Edmond looked like he'd stepped out of a grave, and not because of the beating.

"Drop your fucking guns or I shoot him in the head."

"Who the fuck is this?" The tallest of the men, and the one dressed the most like a normal member of society in a black turtleneck and black slacks, tried to peer around the hippie to see Calvin.

Calvin nudged the hippie in the back. "Answer the man."

"I don't know." The hippie spewed words quickly, spurred on by the gun at his skull. "He was outside. Richie wasn't there. He knows we're here after the old man."

"Here's what happened to Richie." Calvin tossed the cowboy hat forward. The two men facing him saw the bullet hole in their friend's tell tale hat and their faces fell. Calvin assumed the hippie had a similar reaction. He felt the kid's twitching increase.

"Now drop the goddamn guns or I drop this guy."

The man in the turtleneck said, "Richie's dead?"

The hippie didn't like the delay. "For fuck's sake, Joey, do what he says. He's gonna fucking shoot me."

Joey looked at his partner and they both slowly set their guns on the table in front of Edmond who looked dazed.

"Good," Calvin said. "Mr. Stanley, are you okay?"

"Huh?" Edmond looked toward the doorway with unfocused eyes. Calvin figured he couldn't see him around his prisoner. With the two men disarmed he leaned out and showed himself to the room.

"Edmond, are you okay? It's me, Calvin McGraw."

"McGraw?"

Calvin didn't sense any recognition. Could have been that way before these men showed up, or they could have beaten it out of him.

"Make you feel good to beat an old man?" Calvin asked.

"We're just following orders," Joey said.

"You know that's what the Nazis used to say, right?"

"The fuck does that have to do with anything?"

"Shut up." Calvin addressed Edmond again. "Mr. Stanley, come on, sir. You're coming with me. Were gonna get you some place safe."

"There is no place safe," Joey said.

Calvin swept the feet out from under the hippie and he sat hard on the kitchen floor, immediately whining in pain and grabbing as his ass. He took a step forward with the gun outstretched.

"Don't make me shoot you. I don't want to have to shoot you. Really, I don't. But you keep up with your mouth like that and I will and it's gonna be your goddamn fault"

Edmond stood and wobbled to the counter behind him like he was lost.

Joey held his hands up, his throat moving with difficult swallows as his eyes were focused on the barrel of the gun.

"We're gonna leave and then you're gonna leave after us," Calvin said. "You're gonna drive back to Nebraska and tell Cantrell to stop this shit. This is a war you cannot win. You've driven through this state and yours, right? Nothing but space. Plenty of room for both of us. So get back on your side of the fence, okay pal."

Joey looked like he was gearing up to say something, but

Edmond turned around from the counter with a steak knife in his hand. He slashed out at Joey in a jerky movement. The blade cut across the sleeve of his turtleneck and bit through to flesh. Joey cried out and leaned away, bumping his partner who backed into the fridge.

The hippie on the floor thought the apocalypse had come and started screaming as he crawled toward nothing across the kitchen floor.

"Dammit, Edmond," Calvin said. He had this under control, but now this. Calvin stepped forward and put the toe of his boot to the hippie's temple. The long hair went down flat on his belly.

Joey reached up and put a hand on Edmond wrist as he went for a second slash. The old man couldn't power past the younger man's grip and lost the battle for the knife. Joey turned Edmond's hand and pushed. The steak knife went in to Edmond's right side between two ribs high up on his chest.

Calvin fired. Joey's knee exploded and he fell. The partner was trying to push through the wall with nowhere else to go. Calvin shot him in the leg to immobilize him. Caught him higher up on his thigh than he'd meant to. Calvin felt a strange compulsion to apologize to the man for nearly shooting his nuts off, but he didn't.

Edmond fell back against the counter letting a slow wheeze out through his bloody mouth. The knife jutted from his ribs, rammed in nearly up to the hilt.

The hippie was on the move again and Calvin gave him another boot to the head as he crossed the kitchen to help Edmond. Calvin put an arm under his left shoulder and moved him out of the room. The three men left behind were all moaning or screeching about their pain to one another.

Edmond leaned hard on Calvin's shoulder like a KO'd

fighter. His feet shuffled across the floor until Calvin was mostly pulling him along.

"You're gonna be all right, Mr. Stanley."

Calvin doubted the old man had any idea what was happening. He cursed himself for not getting there five minutes earlier. As they passed by the sedan he could hear Richie in the trunk pounding to get out. Calvin leaned Edmond on the car for a moment, reached into his pocket and took out the sedan keys. He threw them as far as he could down the side of the hill, then turned and banged three times on the trunk, shouting, "Shut up."

Calvin hoisted Edmond again and they made their way to the Buick.

Calvin belted the old man in place, leaning him away from the door so he wouldn't fall against it and drive the steak knife any deeper, though there didn't look to be any deeper it could go.

Edmond bled steadily from his chest wound. He sounded like he couldn't get a breath. His lips were pale where they weren't crusted in blood running from his nose.

"McGraw," Edmond wheezed.

Calvin kept his eyes on the road. "Yeah, that's me. You used to run with my father."

"Shit...you're Edgar's boy?" A bloody-toothed grin came to the old man.

"Yessir. Calvin." He steered the Buick around a sharp turn, trying to take it as smooth as he could without sacrificing speed. "I'm gonna get you to some help, okay?"

"Goddamn McGraws," Edmond said, lost in some far off memory. "Always driving a damn car."

Calvin smiled. "That's us."

17

Dorothy knew it was too early for her daily drink so ice cream would have to do. The TV played *General Hospital* in the den with the volume turned up. This was Dorothy's way of not having to admit to herself she watched a soap opera. For her, it was practically a radio hour. She only saw the actor's faces when she passed through the room, but she could still tell you every plot point and scandal plaguing the hospital halls.

In between bites of ice cream she sifted through the day's mail. Nothing interesting there. She thought about adding a few items to the grocery list magneted to the refrigerator when the doorbell rang.

She wiped her mouth on a napkin and went to the door. She'd pulled the door open an inch when it was kicked in and knocked her down. She fell on her shoulder as the TV played along, someone saying, "Doctor, she needs help," in dramatic fashion.

Two men bull rushed in. Both thick across the chest, dark complexions and misshapen noses. They were either brothers or trained at the same boxing gym. Dorothy looked up from the floor and noticed a gun in each man's hand.

"Get up." The man first through the door spoke in a low

growl. Dorothy obeyed his command. When she got upright he pushed the gun in her face.

"Where's your husband?"

Her face felt hot and she pushed back tears. She knew crying wouldn't help her situation.

"He's not here."

"I said where is he."

"I don't know. He doesn't tell me where he goes."

There was no point in lying, saying he sold insurance or something. She trusted everyone in the room knew why they were there.

The gunman looked around the room. He nodded to his partner who went off to check the house. "When's he coming back?"

"I'm not sure."

This was odd. It was crazy. Calvin drove cars. Yes, he worked for the Stanleys, but he didn't get involved in this side of the business. This was never supposed to happen. Then Dorothy thought back to Calvin leaving the house that morning, telling her to be cautious. He knew this was a possibility before he left. He knew more than he was telling her.

The partner came back into the room. "Nobody here."

The TV blared on like a loud conversation at a party. "I'm afraid she's not who she says she is," one character said, followed by a swell of organ music and a commercial for dishwashing liquid.

"Turn that shit off," the commander said. His partner ran over and pulled the plug, then kicked the TV off its stand.

Dorothy felt weak in her legs, unsure how long she could stand still with a gun pointed at her.

"What did he do to you?"

"Nothing. Shut up." The lead gunman seemed to be thinking of a plan. He appeared to have difficulty with the stress on his brain. "When's he coming back?"

"I told you I don't know. May I sit down?"

"Fuck." He kicked backward with his foot, slamming the door closed with a crash that made Dorothy jump. "Sit," he said, pointing to the couch with his gun.

Dorothy used the short walk to the sofa to silently count to ten and to take slow, steady breaths. She needed to be calm. What she didn't want was to be a victim. Her father hadn't wanted that of her and taught her how to fight. Calvin hadn't wanted it either and taught her how to fight dirty. So Dorothy McGraw—early forties, housewife, *General Hospital* fan— bided her time looking for an opening.

Calvin wasn't the only specialist on the Stanley payroll. It had been a good run in the last few years. Very little call for a doctor. But they kept one or two on the books just in case, and they'd never been needed more than now.

The Buick traced a well practiced route to Doc Moller's place. Like a cop on a firing range, Calvin kept certain routes fresh in his muscle memory even if he hadn't needed them in years. A few ways out of town, the way to a safe house if shit got really bad, and the path to Doc Moller's.

Edmond had gone quiet by the time Calvin parked. Not a good sign. He had to rock Edmond like waking him from a nap.

"Edmond," he said loud into his ear. The old man groaned and moved slow as a tortoise. Good enough. Calvin went around to the passenger side and opened the door carefully so Edmond wouldn't spill out onto the ground, maybe push that steak knife all the way through the other side.

He'd managed to avoid getting blood on him so far, but that ended when he bent down to get an arm over Edmond's shoulder and lifted his nearly dead weight. He took a quick look at the dark stains on his Buick's new interior before shutting the door.

Doc Moller squinted at Edmond when he saw them standing on the back step.

"Is that Edmond Stanley?"

"It is, Doc. And that there is a steak knife in his ribs. Can we get this thing moving?"

"This way."

The Doc stepped aside and Calvin dragged the old man down the hall in Moller's house to a room fitted like an operating room. A redhead in a white nurse's outfit came in, saw Edmond and asked of the Doc, "Should I send Mrs. Campbell home?"

"Tell her I'll call on her later at home. This might take some doing."

Calvin leaned Edmond onto the table but by then he was spent and the old man slid out of his hands and flopped like a drunk pig and made similar noises. He managed to keep the knife from getting rolled on or going any deeper into Edmond's side.

Doc Moller didn't ask what happened. He, like Calvin, knew better. Do the job, don't ask unnecessary questions, get paid and go away quiet.

Calvin watched as the Doc examined the knife up close and personal, tearing away the shirt to get a better look at the surrounding area. Calvin could see tiny bubbles in the blood around the knife. Air leaking from Edmond's lung.

The Doc gathered supplies on a stainless steel tray and pulled on thin gloves, but no mask. The redhead reentered the OR and brushed past Calvin like he wasn't there.

"It's in pretty deep, Cal. I think I might need a firmer hand for the extraction."

"I'll wash the area," she said and set about cleaning the skin and dried blood from around the protruding knife. Doc Moller looked up at Calvin.

"You're up."

"What do you mean?"

"Pull the knife out when I say go."

Calvin went pale. He was supposed to stay in the car. Keep the engine running. Hands at ten and two. Not this bullshit.

"I'm not a doctor," he said.

"You don't need to be, just gotta have a firm grip." Doc gathered up what he needed to slip in a chest tube and re-inflate the lung once the knife was out. He looked at Calvin again, waiting. Calvin stepped forward. He reached out slowly and wrapped a fist around the knife. The handle was sticky with blood.

"Okay," Doc Moller said. "One...Two..."

"Hold on," Calvin said.

"What?"

"I thought you were going to say go."

Doc rolled his eyes at Calvin, sighed, and started again. "Ready...set...go."

Calvin pulled. The knife resisted more than he expected so he bore down on it and pulled harder. Those ribs really had a grip and he set a hand on Edmond's chest and pushed while he pulled with the other hand. The knife jerked out in one swift motion, followed by a gusher of blood. Edmond was passed out by now.

Doc Moller went to work and ignored Calvin, calling out orders to the redhead who handed him what he needed. Calvin slowly backed out and went to sit in the waiting room, the knife still in his blood-soaked hand.

Dorothy didn't like the nervous jump in his knee.

The partner wouldn't keep still, but his pacing had been slow and repetitive. She bet he was regretting kicking over the TV about now. But the man in charge, he was a ball of nerves. A rubber band stretched tight. In his collection of nervous ticks, Dorothy could see him squeezing off a shot from his .38 without realizing it.

She was tired of waiting for an opportunity. Time to create one.

"I told you I didn't know when he'd be back."

The gunman gave her a stare from under his sweaty brow. "We can wait."

"I don't know for how long."

His pent-up anger burst. "I said we can wait." He kicked out with his foot, flipping the coffee table and tossing the small pile of magazines and the glass grapes centerpiece. Dorothy tensed, then waited until the room was quiet again before breathing out.

She gave them an out, but they wanted to play it this way. She took a breath, careful to draw the air in slowly and let it out easy, not in a big attention-getting huff. She needed to steady her nerves and keep the appearance of calm.

"I don't know about you," she said, "but I could use a drink."

The partner perked up. "A drink sounds good, Lou."

Lou wiped a hand across his forehead. The sweat there was thick with worry, his stink filling the room. "Yeah, I guess I could go for a drink."

"I keep a bottle hidden from my husband. He doesn't like me drinking, but since you boys are being nice, I'll share with you, okay?"

"Lady, if you think this is being nice I'd hate to see what your husband does to you."

"Look, Lou...can I call you Lou?" He nodded. "When you came in here I thought you'd try to rape me or kill me. But you've been good to me. I know my husband's business. I know what this is all about. I guess part of me figured it would happen someday. So here it is and I need a drink just as bad as you do. Maybe more." She watched him closely, searching for signs her voice hadn't betrayed her panic.

Lou nodded along, proud of himself in her eyes. "So quit yapping and get us a drink."

There she was. Step number two. Establish trust. Step number one had been to listen to her husband when he left. Dorothy went to her linen cabinet under the partner's watchful eye. She knew they'd never make their own drinks while there was a woman in the room to do it for them. So far, they'd been easy to predict.

Up and moving it was easier to hide her shakes. She reached behind the towels to where her bottle of bourbon hid, and also where she'd stashed the gun Calvin made her keep for emergencies. Emergencies that had never come up until today.

"I'll get some glasses. Do you want ice?" She set the bottle in her left hand, kept her right inside the cabinet. Under the towels her hand found the gun.

"We don't need no ice," the partner said.

"Okay. You first." She tossed the bottle. She threw it underhand, high, arcing toward his chin. His eyes focused on the bourbon. His hands went up, gun hand too. Dorothy's hand came out from under the towels. She set her feet, assumed a two-handed grip and fired for center mass. Two shots hit him—one in the chest, one in the belly. The bottle bounced off his forehead as he went down.

The sound jolted Lou from his seat. Dorothy was already on the move. She pressed against the doorway to the kitchen, her shoulder resting on the last pencil mark of Webb's growth chart marked there from when he was thirteen and nearly as tall as her.

The gutshot man howled in pain. Lou took shelter behind the chair, unsure where the shots came from and unwilling to believe it had been Dorothy. She knew she needed to act fast. She didn't want a shootout with him. A few weekends of paper targets wouldn't match up to a career criminal. Surprise was her only advantage.

"The fuck you do that for?" Lou bellowed.

"Jesus. Oh, sweet Jesus," the partner said. Dorothy could see him writhing on the floor, soaking blood into her carpet. He kept putting his hands to his gut and checking the blood on them. He wiped his palms on his shirt, on his pants, then put them back to his wounds and bloodied them again.

Dorothy squatted behind the doorway having second thoughts. She should have waited for Calvin to come home. But then they were going to kill him as soon as he walked in the door. She stewed over his not being there. She got angry at his little hint from that morning. He knew something. At least he knew she would listen to him.

No, Dorothy was the last woman to become a victim, but

she felt like a victim of the Stanleys right then. Whoever Lou and his partner were, she knew it was the Stanley boys—not Calvin—who brought them to her door.

The sensible man would gather his wounded friend and leave. Lou demonstrated his lack of sense by firing three rapid shots at the empty doorway. Two bullets went through the linen closet door and one pierced the wall.

"You boys better get the hell out of my house." Dorothy made her voice loud and commanding. "Your friend is hurt bad there. You'd best get him some attention."

"Bitch, all you had to do was sit still and wait," Lou said.

"McGraws don't sit still and wait for anybody."

Dorothy slid out in a crouch, pivoting her body around the doorframe. She fired twice at Calvin's favorite chair. Puffs of filling appeared like blood spray around the holes. Lou grunted and noise of pain and annoyance. Dorothy took cover again.

Lou stood and fired. Blood leaked down the side of his head from a crescent shaped tear in his ear. His bullets found the blank wall again. Six shots, Dorothy counted. She listened and heard shell casings hit the stone hearth of the fireplace. Lou was reloading.

Dorothy thought the words in her head then reconsidered and said them out loud, but to herself. In case this was a terrible idea, she wanted them to be her last words.

"I love you, Cal."

She kicked off her shoes, stood, raised the gun in front of her and marched forward. She knew there wasn't much time. The man at the gun range had showed her a speed loader. Lou might have one of those. She wanted to make her shots count, but couldn't wait too long to use them. In her path was the partner, gone silent with pain and his movements slowing.

She saw Lou's shadow against the wall, but she couldn't see his body behind the chair and the short side table where Calvin always forgot to put his Pabst on a coaster. Dozens of interlocking rings decorated the top of that little wooden rectangle.

Her stocking feet moved silently over the carpet. She heard what sounded like the chamber of the revolver snap into place. She had to shoot now or she'd be making herself a paper target for Lou. She estimated where he was behind the chair and fired twice more. Two more wounds blossomed in the fabric and Lou yowled in pain. Her gun clicked on an empty chamber.

Lou was scrambling behind the chair. He sounded like a dog trying to gain footing on a linoleum floor. He wasn't dead. He was pissed. His cry of pain turned into a howl of rage. She saw a leg appear from behind the chair, then an arm swung around. He was hurt, obviously, but determined now to inflict his own pain on her.

Dorothy kept moving forward. She didn't know why, only that she knew it was what Calvin would do. She bent and picked up the partner's gun from beside his bloody hand. He wasn't moving any more.

Lou's first shot went over her head, right where she'd been standing a second ago. She saw him through the legs of the overturned coffee table. She stayed low, got her two-handed grip on the new gun and fired. Lou fell back, a spatter of blood on the fireplace stones. He made no sound. As she got closer she could see where her shot took out most of the left side of his head.

She immediately fell to tears. She put a hand to her mouth and then jumped when she realized it held a gun. She dropped the stranger's gun and took a step back, tears smearing her vision and mercifully blotting out the view of Lou's dead body.

She kicked something with her heel and turned to see the bottle of bourbon, unbroken, resting on the carpet. She let herself cry for another half minute, then picked up the bottle and drank straight from the neck.

18

Webb quickly discovered Big Dan to be a bit of a legend along highway 63. Nearly every place he'd stopped had at least heard of Big Dan and many had seen him either last week on his run out to Omaha or three weeks ago on his way back to Arkansas or even a month or two ago when he passed by the same way he'd been doing for nearly two decades.

More than one person asked, "He owe you money?"

Webb figured he'd make it seem like he was someone Big Dan wanted to see so he answered, "No, in fact I owe him a little. Wanted to see he got it back."

More than a few people were skeptical of that tale—who goes out of their way to pay back money?—and some hinted at Big Dan's side business. "If you're lookin' to buy I can set you up."

Webb declined all offers and moved on down the road.

Outside Eldon, Missouri, Webb found a truck stop proprietor with a bald head and all of three teeth on his upper side.

"Yeah, I seen him today."

Webb lit up. "Is he staying around here?"

"Nah, he's just droppin' off." The bald man wiped a line

of spittle off his chin. "Gotta forgive me. Forgot to put in my uppers this mornin'." He wiped again. "But like I said, Big Dan he made his delivery so I got you set for whatever it is you're lookin' fer."

It seemed that Dan was transporting more than car parts across state lines. Common knowledge went that truckers always did have the best speed.

"Got a load of Bennies," the bald man said. He scratched at his clean skull trying to remember what else was in the load beyond Benzedrine. "Got some powder you sniff up yer nose and it makes you run all night and stiffens up yer pecker too."

Webb ignored the shopping list. With a stop in Omaha Big Dan might have even been transporting for Cantrell. That's not what Webb needed at all.

"Did he have a girl with him? A blonde?"

Baldy showed his three yellowed teeth. His tongue bobbed in and out of the gaps, purple and swollen. "You got to see Big Dan direct for that. He don't make deliveries on the girls no more. Not after what happened in '66."

Webb wanted to know, but didn't really.

"You want one of Big Dan's girls you gotta go to the Royal Club outside of Lake Ozark. That's where he runs 'em at. But if you want a girl we got a gal named Henrietta workin' out of the back of the bait shop who'll treat you real nice. Ten bucks'll get you in the back door."

Webb didn't like the sound of "Big Dan's girls" one bit.

"You know what way he went from here?"

"South, I suspect." Baldy got a skeptical crinkle in his brow. Any man who's truly horny always took up the offer for Henrietta. Webb seemed to have a one track mind for Big Dan, not his girls or his drugs. "What'd you say yer name was?"

Webb turned toward the door. "James Hendrix. I'm obliged to you." And he was gone.

His dad always said driving was the best way to clear your head. It wasn't working.

Of course, Calvin said driving was the best way to cure most of what ailed you.

For Webb, the Eliminator was far from a hammock on the beach. His hands were tense on the wheel. His ass was sweaty in the seat. The engine noise, Calvin's favorite part, grated on him like a jazz song. A collection of metal sounds, that's all it was. No melody.

Dad would beat his ass more for saying that than for losing the girl.

Joni. What the hell was she thinking? She'd suckered him and he could see now that it was a long con. Started the minute she got in the car. Probably before. She was a liar and a fake. Probably all that shit she was saying about Hugh Stanley was bullshit too. But Webb knew she was right.

Webb saw a sign for the Ozark Lakes ahead. Beautiful country all around him, but all he could see were sharp branches and dead leaves and a lake like a black pit of sludge. Joni was here somewhere and he started to feel like she was going to need saving from her own dumb idea.

Rescue her from one man to deliver her to another. Webb shook it off and kept driving.

Doc Moller removed his glasses and sat down next to Calvin with a sigh.

"He'll make it if we can keep getting blood into him. I

don't keep that much on hand. He's gotta go to the hospital."

"But he's gonna make it?"

"Most likely. I don't make guarantees."

A good way to go through life, Calvin thought.

"You need me to take him?" Calvin was rising and reaching in his pocket for keys.

"No, no, sit down." Doc Moller patted the air, motioning Calvin to sit. "Ambulance is on its way."

Cal exhaled. His job was done, then.

"And I called Hugh, filled him in," Doc Moller said.

"Thanks, Doc."

"They pay me for it same as you."

He pat Calvin's knee twice and stood. Calvin looked through a thin opening into the operating room. Edmond was laid out, eyes closed, looking for all the world like he was dead except for the slow and shallow rise and fall of his chest.

19

Calvin had never come home to Dorothy with a gun in her hand before. The look in her red-rimmed eyes frightened him more.

"What happened?"

She stood, didn't let go of the gun, and wrapped her arms around him. Calvin held his wife while she cried. He didn't ask again until he knew she was ready. By then he had seen the bodies in the living room, the overturned table, the smashed TV.

She told him the story. He could tell she was a little drunk and he didn't blame her a bit. He eased the gun from her hand, set it on the kitchen counter and put on the Mr. Coffee.

"You knew about it," she said.

Calvin turned. "What? I didn't know about this, what are you talking about?"

"You warned me. You knew this might happen."

Calvin ran a hand over his face, his palm scratching on the stubble building on his chin.

"Thinking it might happen and knowing it would are two different things." He studied her expression. Unconvinced. "You're absolutely right. I knew it might. I should have never left you here alone."

"When the Stanleys call..."

"Fuck them. I quit. Right now, this is over."

Dorothy saw he was doing the coffee wrong. She came over to finish it properly. Giving her hands something to do helped.

"It wasn't Stanley men who came here tonight," she said.

"No, it wasn't." Calvin's turn to tell a story. "There's another organization over in Nebraska. They want to move in and naturally Hugh and Vic don't want that to happen."

"How did they end up here?"

"I guess they know about me. We've... had some run-ins lately."

"And you weren't planning on telling me." Dorothy crossed her arms across her chest.

"I didn't want to worry you. It's a bullshit turf war and I didn't think it would get to this. But I'm serious. I'm done. I'll go tell Hugh right now if—"

"No." She moved toward him again, putting a hand on his arm to keep him from leaving. She looked like a child and he pulled her into another hug.

"I don't want you to quit," she said. "Not yet at least."

"What do you want, Dot? What would make you happy? Safe?"

She pulled away and looked up at him with his arms still around her back. "I want you to get those mother fuckers."

Calvin glanced into the living room. Seemed like she'd already done the job, but he knew what she meant. All the way to the top. End this war and end the threat.

"Besides," she said. "We can't go anywhere without Webb."

"About that..."

She broke from from his embrace. "Jesus Christ, Cal, I don't know if I can take much more."

"He's okay," he reassured her. "He's a little bit in the weeds on his first job. He kind of... lost the cargo."

"He what? How'd he do that?"

"She did a runner on him. But he's on it. He's smart and he'll find her."

"Her? What the hell is he doing?"

"Bringing back a runaway. It's not dangerous at all."

"Unless he doesn't find her." She knew the deal.

Calvin put his hands on her waist, looked her in the eye. "He will. He's a McGraw. And look at what we're capable of." He turned his head to the carnage in the next room.

Her face was flooded with memories. "My god, Cal, can't you do something about them."

"I'll take care of it. You sit here and have your coffee." He almost told her to watch some TV, but that option was gone. He started toward the garage to get supplies for the cleanup. He stopped and turned back to her. "You really don't want me to quit?"

"A McGraw don't quit on a fight. And they brought the fight to our door. You go get 'em."

"There's not a day goes by I'm not reminded why I married you."

Webb parked the Eliminator at the far end of a gravel lot outside the Royal Club. When he got out, the smell of the lake came on strong. Rotted leaves and frogs and the green slime that grows on stagnant water. Mosquitoes buzzed around like they owned the air.

The Royal had corrugated tin walls, a roof pieced together

by what looked like scraps of lumber but may have been the result of years of patches slowly replacing all the original wood. A few hundred empty beer bottles and fifths of Jack Daniel's littered the banks of the lake out behind the club where they'd been lazily dumped. A hand painted sign read WATCH OUT FOR SNAKES.

One other car and two pickup trucks were parked in the lot. No big rigs. Webb went inside.

Three ceiling fans turned lazy circles and moved no air whatsoever around the dim and stale room. A slow blues played on the jukebox or stereo, Webb wasn't sure which. It added to the sadness of the day drinkers inside. Two solitary men at opposite ends of the bar, each intent on doing their drinking alone and uninterrupted.

The bartender was a man with a massive beer gut stuffed into a cutoff sleeveless T-shirt in black with a faded confederate flag. He sported a thick black mustache that completely hid his lips from view. Webb went to the bar and leaned on the brass rail.

"Beer?" the barman said.

"Yeah. Bottle."

"I got cans. Stroh's, Dixie, Schmidt, Hamm's."

"Hamm's."

Fresh from a cooler under the bar, the beer was cold. The barman didn't set down a coaster. Bowls of salty peanuts were placed every other stool along the bar. A jar of pickled eggs sat nearest the door. Webb wondered how often the brine got changed out.

"I'm looking for Big Dan," Webb said.

The barman said, "He ain't here just now," and rang a bell just under the bar top, the kind Webb used to hear in school when homeroom started. Across the room a curtain pushed aside and three women walked slowly into the main room of the club like their coffee break had been interrupted. They were surly and sour, but dressed like an Ozark interpretation of a French boudoir. Frilly lace, clasps and straps, cleavage and high cut panties. Nothing else.

Webb asking about Big Dan prompted a sampling of his goods. Webb breathed a small sigh of relief that none of the girls were Joni.

The barman didn't do any selling. He let the girls lineup and stand, bored out of their beehived heads. Two of the three chewed gum. Not that it would clean out the residue of whatever they'd had in their mouths before.

"You want my advice," the barman said. "Ginny is the way to go. One on the end." He winked and nodded in her direction. Webb looked her over and she, like the others, looked like forty miles of bad road.

Webb knew he had to play the part if he wanted to find Big Dan.

"I was kinda hoping for some fresher meat, you know what I mean? I heard tell Big Dan was traveling with some new talent."

The barman waved a hand at the girls and they all shuffled back to their curtain, annoyed they had to come out for nothing.

"You mean the blondie? He's got her working a special right now, but she be back soon." He smiled and Webb could make out stained teeth behind the wall of whiskers.

The beer turned in his stomach to think Joni was already being pimped out. If she was the blonde he spoke of. Big Dan may have already dropped her off at some other club next to

135

a rancid swamp higher up on the highway. By the time Webb get her back to Mr. Stanley he might not want damaged goods like that.

But she wasn't goods. Webb knew her too well now. He wanted her back for himself first, Hugh Stanley second. For the Stanleys he'd try to find her. For himself, he would hunt.

"A special, huh? What's that, like a house call?"

The barman seemed eager for conversation, getting none as he was from the two lonely drinkers at the bar.

"Sometimes you get married men who don't like to come down here. A few high rollers, you know. Big Dan he plays all the angles, man. You want it, he can get it."

"So I've heard."

The barman pointed to Webb's beer. "You want another one?"

"Nah. I'm a slow drinker. Besides, looks like I'll have to wait."

Calvin was filthy and still had the blood to clean off his living room floor. The two bodies he'd dumped in the old trash furnace at the back of the property. The twelve foot pit hadn't been used in a decade and he'd considered filling it in, but never got around to it. Now he'd have to think about pouring some concrete down there, making a mausoleum out of it, minus the names etched into the side. He didn't know who the hell the two men he'd buried were, only who they worked for and that he felt glad they were dead.

Seeing Dorothy's handiwork made him doubt his own reluctance to get lethal in his work. Letting those men live out on the highway with Kirby had led to him being on Cantrell's list. That's what he got for having an ounce of mercy in a merciless business.

The blood smearing his clothes had turned dark as the dirt and ten-year-old soot. He clapped his hands and wiped them on his pants but they still looked like photos he'd seen of coal miners. Honest, working man's hands. Calvin had grown callouses from gripping a wheel so many years. Even after he adopted driving gloves a few years back he still had rough palms, but nothing like the hard skin of a real working man. He'd met men in town who worked at the lumber mill or who worked construction or out on the highway crew. All of them put palms of rough hewn canvas into his hands to shake and Calvin always felt inferior in some way.

Bet none of them ever dumped two bodies down a hole as a favor to their wives, though.

As he stepped through the back door he heard a car pull away fast. A big V8, he could hear. Made for pulling power, not for speed. A heavy car, four door. Heavy muffler meant to disguise the sound of horsepower. He figured Cadillac.

Dorothy was at the front door as if she'd just ushered someone out, or kept someone from coming in, more like.

"Was someone just here?" he asked.

Dorothy held onto the door knob for another few moments like she needed to keep it in her hand to prevent her from punching someone. And Calvin was the only one there.

"As a matter of fact, there was."

"Did they see anything?" Calvin asked, tossing a glance to the blood stained floor. He hadn't set the TV right or the coffee table yet.

"No. I kept them on the front step. She was just here to tell me a few things anyway."

"She? Who was it?"

Dorothy finally turned around, her mouth a tight line. She looked like she wanted her bottle of bourbon back. "Nancy Stanley."

Calvin's face went white, even under the dirt. Nothing good could come of a visit from Nancy.

"What did she want?"

"To get something off her chest is how she put it."

Calvin took a step forward, but not too close. He still couldn't read Dorothy's mood. She was mad for sure, but at whom?

"You gonna tell me what or keep me guessing?"

"She wanted to let me know you and she have been fucking for the past six months. Said it broke her heart to have to be the one to break up such a happy marriage, but thought I should know what a cad I'd married."

"Dot..."

"She said you told her you loved her. She said you wanted to leave me and tried to get her to divorce Victor. She said–"

"It's all bullshit." He took another step forward, still out of swinging range from her hands which were now balled into fists.

Dorothy continued, her volume increasing. "She said she couldn't trust you enough to have a real relationship with you because she knew you'd been lying to me. She wanted to end it but didn't want you to get away with it for another minute. She said she had no idea how many other women you were sleeping with."

"Dorothy, you know it's a lie. All of it. You *know* that."

Her eyes brimmed with fresh tears. He could see her grinding her teeth. She smiled, let go a derisive huff and wiped her eyes with her clenched fists.

"I know it's a lie, Cal. She's a goddamn nutcase. I know you'd never step out on me and I damn sure know you wouldn't do it with that witch."

Calvin felt his whole body go loose. "Sweet goddamn, Dot, you had me worried you believed her shit."

"Calvin, you are a lot of nasty shit, but you are not a cheater. Not on me, anyways."

He rushed across the room and grabbed her in a hug, smearing her with dirt and dried blood but neither one cared. "I told you she was a fucking psycho."

"You got that right. She stood there and wept real tears of shame. Well, she ought to be ashamed."

"When is this gonna friggin' end?"

Dorothy pulled back, looked him in the eye. "I think you need to end it, Cal."

"We got more problems than any sensible man can handle right now."

"That's the truth of it."

Calvin felt the relief of Dorothy believing him subside and the rush of hot anger over what Nancy had tried to do flood over him. That bitch. Tried to bring down his marriage just because he told her no. She was as goddamn dangerous as the men who busted into his house, nearly.

And it was a goddamn distraction he did not need with life and death pressures on his head. He also knew it was one problem he could take care of quickly and easily. The plan was already in place.

"I have to tell Vic yes, don't I?"

"Something needs to be done about her."

"No telling what she'll do next when she sees this little plan of hers didn't work."

"Maybe she comes back here with a gun she keeps in *her* linen closet," Dorothy said. "If she can't get me to leave on my own, maybe she takes me out of the way."

Calvin didn't know if she was merely justifying Vic's plan or if she'd gone paranoid now that someone had tried to kill her—and him. Once you see it as a possibility, every knock on the door could be the boogeyman.

"Vic sure made it sound like I didn't have a choice in the matter."

"Calvin," she said. "I'm sick and tired of people coming to my door trying to ruin my life. I want my son back, I want my life back. If that means staying with the Stanleys or leaving I don't much care anymore. You've always said to me I married an outlaw. Well, Calvin McGraw, go be an outlaw."

Calvin kissed her hard on the lips. He felt like a gas pedal had been pressed to the floor. His heart sped up and his eyesight sharpened. Time to get behind the wheel of his own damn life again. This passenger shit wasn't where a McGraw is meant to be.

20

Webb gave in and ordered a second beer. He turned his back to the bar and leaned on his elbows. The blues on the stereo kept slinging hard luck stories supposed to make you feel better because the singer's life was worse than yours. Webb knew he had them beat.

Two guys came in. Skinny country boys in cutoff plaid shirts and cowboy boots with mud in the seams. They went and sat at a table. The barman dinged his bell and the girls came out of the back. The guys made a few side jokes to themselves, pent-up with nervous energy, then each made their selections. The leftover girl looked relieved to have not been picked.

When everyone disappeared behind the curtain again the barman brought Webb his fresh beer.

"Last can of Hamm's I got."

"I'll be sure to enjoy it."

Webb pointed to a box in the corner, a sort of pen about six foot by six foot. Reminded him of the sandbox he used to play in over at his grandfather's house, only this one had a grid of painted numbers—ten across and ten up and down making a hundred little squares.

"What's that?" he asked.

"We use that for the chicken drop on Saturday nights."

"Chicken drop?"

"You ain't never heard of a chicken drop?"

"Would I be asking?"

The barman set a foot on a shelf behind the bar and explained with a certain Ozark pride in the game they came up with.

"Y'see, you got a hundred squares in there, each one's got a number on it. You pay a dollar per square. Then we put a chicken in there. Let him walk around a while. But y'see, the chicken, just 'fore he went in the box, they feed him some of Deke's chili, see? Real hot with Tabasco sauce and shit in it. Well, everyone sets around hootin' and hollerin' and hoping that chicken is going shit on their number. He does, you win the money. Get it now?"

"Chicken drop," Webb said, eyeing the box. "Huh."

The barman did a little drum run on the bar top with his hands and looked like he couldn't wait for Saturday night, then he moved off down the bar.

Now, Webb knew engines. Not as well as his daddy, but he knew them better than most, and what pulled into the gravel lot next was a big rig. Air brakes hissed and the engine shut down. Webb braced himself for what he hoped would be Big Dan, then realized he had no idea what he'd do if it was. He took a gulp of beer for courage.

A beer keg gut preceded the man into the room by a good two seconds. Behind a belt buckle strained to the max was a man who fit the Big description, that was for sure. With a side to side waddle the man wedged his girth through the door and let it swing back so the person behind him had to block the door from hitting her in the face. It was Joni.

She looked haunted, like she'd just come out of the dark and her eyes hadn't adjusted yet. She walked in a shuffle behind him, her head down toward the floor. She didn't see Webb at the bar. She wasn't looking for him. She wasn't looking for anything or toward anything. She seemed like to look up would be to see into the future and her future was dark as the bottom of a fresh dug grave.

Big Dan waved her to move faster. "Come on now." His accent was backwoods thick, his breathing heavy. The rigorous act of crossing the floor had winded him. He pushed her along to where the curtain hung like the gates of hell before her.

Webb didn't know what to do. He was frozen in place, watching the object of his hunt walk right by him. Big Dan was fat, out of shape, sweaty and with some sort of sore on his mouth, yet somehow Webb was intimidated. Hearing all about his reputation up and down the highway had put the man on some sort of pedestal for Webb. A steel reinforced pedestal, but still. Chances were good he had people working for him. Maybe the barman or the other two patrons who hadn't moved except to lift their beers since Webb came in.

Surely there was muscle behind the curtain to keep the girls safe. Or maybe the girl's protection was low on the priority list. Girl got too beat up, just nab a new one off the highway in Iowa.

Webb looked down at his hand and noticed he had crushed the beer can in his fist. Foam leaked over the sides like his anger boiling over in him.

He needed to get Joni back, but to do that he'd need to take a run at Big Dan. To do *that* he'd need something more than his fists. He felt like punching Big Dan in the gut would be the same as sinking his arms up to the elbows in unset cement. But what could he use?

Webb knew every joint in America had some weaponry behind the bar. Might be a gun, might be a baseball bat. This deep in the Ozarks he expected a sawed off, maybe something double barreled that shot rabid water moccasins instead of bullets. Whatever it was he had to get at it.

Webb slurped the rest of his beer that hadn't spilled and flagged down the barman.

"Another Hamm's."

"You got my last."

"Can you go check? Hamm's was my daddy's brand. We lost him last month. Makes me think of him even just to see the can." He held up his crushed can. The barman wasn't sure if Webb might end up drinking himself off the deep end or if this was a solid deep south way to honor your fallen father.

"I can check the cooler in back."

"You do that and my daddy would be mighty obliged to you."

The barman took a look around the room. "Ain't exactly happy hour I suppose." He stepped out around the homemade bar top, then turned to Webb. "Hey, wasn't you waiting for Big Dan? That was him just come in here toting his new blonde."

"I was, then I got to thinkin' about my daddy and I fell out of the mood, you know?"

"Yeah. I get it." The barman pushed through a screen door that whined like a sick cat before slapping shut with a sound like the hand of God smacking a mosquito off the ass of the world.

He went out of the room and Webb went to work. He ducked down and scurried around the edge of the bar on the

144

far end closest to the door. The two day drinkers didn't seem to notice or didn't pay him any mind if they did. Webb stayed hunched down as he moved along the bar back. He saw extra glasses, rags, a cash box held together with rubber bands, a few bottles of the good stuff, several baggies of weed, spare jars of pickled pigs feet, a mounted alligator head that wasn't on the wall for some reason. But no gun. At the very far end he saw a lead pipe on a hook. It was about the length of his arm and it looked like it would do the job.

Webb duck walked toward it. He heard a door slap shut. God slapping another skeeter. Webb was too far from the pipe. If he went for it, he'd be caught and he'd never make it as far as Big Dan. He retreated fast, shimmying around the end of the bar and popping up to see the barman's confused face.

"Had to tie my shoe," he said.

"Well, like I said. No more Hamm's. How about a Dixie?"

"You know what, I changed my mind again. Think I'll go grab me a piece of that blonde."

The barman shook his head watching the indecisive customer go.

Webb reached the curtain and drew a deep breath. When his dad described the virtues of the McGraw job he always emphasized that they stayed in the safety of the car. No gun play. No dangerous outings. Just drive, that's all. Right then he felt as safe as if he'd put his skull under a tire and dropped a brick on the gas pedal.

Webb pushed through the curtain.

He found himself in a short hallway. Red-tinted light came from a room at the end. Each of the four doors along the corridor were closed. He could hear the rutting of the two skinny country boys coming from two rooms. They wasted no time.

He walked forward and came to the doorless doorway. Big Dan was there talking with the muscle Webb suspected.

"The fuck?" the muscle said.

"I didn't hear no bell," Big Dan said.

"I'm not here for a girl. I want to talk to Dan." Neither man moved. "About the blonde. Joni."

The muscle reached behind his back for a gun. He held it down at his waist.

"You got an appointment?"

Webb decided do or die. Pretend like you're behind the wheel.

"You know you got stolen property?"

Big Dan grinned. "Issat right?"

"You know the Stanleys out of Iowa City?"

Big Dan's jowls drooped. "She kept saying that name. Who the fuck are they?"

"If you don't know," Webb said, "trust me, you don't want to get to know them like this."

Big Dan wasn't easily intimidated. "Well, what the fuck was she doing down here thumbing for a ride? Sounds to me like finders keepers."

"We can make an arrangement," Webb said. The words were coming easily, but with no plan behind them. Just like being on the road though, keep moving forward is what Calvin always told him. Don't spin your wheels or go in reverse. Don't take your eyes off the road. What's ahead of you is always more dangerous than what's behind.

"What kind of arrangement?"

"The kind that doesn't get you killed."

The muscle took a step forward. "You making threats, boy?"

"You should know..." He hoped the trickle of sweat running down his temple didn't betray him. "You kill me and ten more show up tomorrow and they won't be asking for a parlay."

Big Dan waved a hand for the muscle to stand down. Neither was too sure about Webb, but they weren't willing to dismiss him just yet.

A wild moan came from one of the country boy's rooms.

"Let's step outside where we can talk in quiet. I don't know about you but I don't get off on hearing another man screw."

Big Dan used the edge of a table to haul himself up. The muscle took a step forward.

Webb held out a hand. "Top brass only."

Clearly the muscle didn't care for Webb. Big Dan waved him off. "Keep an eye on the girls. Make sure them two boys paid up. One of them was talking about takin' a trip down the Hershey highway. He does, he owes an extra five."

The floorboards creaked under Dan's weight as he led the way out back of the Royal club. When they were outside the blues were replaced by a chorus of frogs and cicadas in the trees. Stagnant water and mud smells mixed with sour beer from the mountain of empty bottles on the shoreline. The setting sun reflected off the still water and it could have been pretty if the Royal hadn't dropped so much ugly onto the lakeside.

Big Dan slapped at a mosquito feeding off his neck.

"So what's this arrangement? And talk fast, them skeeters is gonna eat us alive and go home fat and happy."

Webb had him alone and didn't know what to do about it. He kept playing his part until inspiration struck.

"A rental fee, let's call it. Twenty-five percent of what she earns."

"Twenty-five, huh?"

"More than fair, given that you swiped her without asking."

Big Dan slapped his neck again. "She kept sayin' to me, Mister Stanley's gonna kill you. Mister Stanley ain't gonna like this one bit."

"No, he is not. But I can make it work."

Dan's feet sunk in the mud of the banks, then slurped out with a sucking sound to rival anything going on in the whore's rooms. He toed around a few bottles. Webb noticed the trees were hung with empty bottles swaying in the breeze and now and then clanking together like hillbilly wind chimes.

"How about I just sell her back to you?"

"Sell her?"

"Yeah. She's a real good 'un. Hate to see her go, but I'm more of a cash on the barrel head type more than a rent by the week type." Slap. Another mosquito down. "She's a real good piece of pussy. I can tell you straight from personal experience on that, my friend."

Plan or not, Webb needed to act. He bent down, picked up a bottle and brought it down over Big Dan's head. Dan wobbled, stunned. Webb picked up another, smashed it over Dan's thick skull again. A line of blood leaked out from Dan greasy hairline. Webb picked up another, smashed it. Then another.

Big Dan fell. He hit the mud and rolled over on the pile of empties causing an avalanche. Big Dan was a beached whale and a flipped tortoise in one. Webb pounced. He got his knees up on Big Dan's back and began pounding empty bottles into him until they broke. After a dozen Dan didn't seem to move.

Webb pushed his face down into the mud on the edge of the dark water. The bottles falling deeper into the lake splashed the algae-strewn water over Dan's head. He resisted, but he was no match for Webb.

Webb ground the fat man's face into the mud, filling his nose and clogging his throat. He took a bottle off the pile and gave one final whack to the back of Dan's head, then slid off and fell back into the pile. Glass crunched under him as he rolled down the stack until he landed in the mud. He sat there catching his breath, watching the sun disappear over the horizon, a fireball snuffed out by the black waters of the lake. He got himself on his feet, lake water heavy in his jeans, and stood back to survey the damage.

No breathing. Blood from every corner of Big Dan's head. The frogs had gone silent, only the mosquitoes buzzed in his ear.

When Webb was ten years old he was out playing in the snow the day after Christmas with his friend Danny. Webb had his brand new Radio Flyer sled set up at the top of the hill and as he turned to ask Danny a question it got away from him. Damn thing slid down the hill so fast it shot out over the gully and launched into the little pond there and sank under the thin ice. Webb remembered Danny's words: "Well, you gone and done it now."

Those words echoed in his head as he stared down at the inert body of Big Dan like a log stuck in the mud at the edge of the lake.

And his work was not done.

Webb turned and walked back inside clutching a broken bottle neck in his fist. He came into the back room where Mr. Muscles sat reading a porn mag. He looked up at Webb like a swamp creature had just stepped into the room.

"The hell happened out there?"

"We came to an agreement," Webb said.

Muscles took in the mud, the blood, the bottle neck. He stood fast and reached around his back. Webb hit the accelerator. He jumped forward, shoved muscles in his chest and knocked him off balance. The gun came out and landed on the couch cushions as Webb chased him down to the ground with the bottle neck leading the way. He pressed it up against Muscle's neck.

"Where's the blonde?"

"The fuck you do to Big Dan?"

He shoved the jagged edge in harder. "You really want to find out?"

"Fuck it. Keep the girl. I don't give a shit."

Webb discovered pressing a man's face into the mud from behind was different from staring him in the eye. He couldn't give the bottle that final push to break skin. He couldn't kill a man while looking at him.

Webb stood, picked up the gun and threw it hard out the open door. He heard it splash into the lake.

"Get out. The back way. Get gone and don't come back."

Muscles didn't have to be asked twice. He stood and ran, his footsteps squishing in the mud as he retreated.

Webb went to the hallway, already regretting his decision not to keep the gun. If he was going to spend more time out of the car, he'd have to get better at it. He approached the first door, kicked it in and found one of the skinny country boys leaning back in bed while his girl worked her mouth on his pecker. He sat up quick and yelled. The girl gagged and came away from his lap about to throw up.

"Get the fuck outta here."

Webb went to the next door, kicked it in and found the second country boy in mid-rut. His white ass cheeks like a sheet of new paper on top of his farmer-tanned legs. Even if he heard the door come in, he didn't stop pumping.

Webb went to the next door and kicked. Joni cowered against the far wall. When she looked up between her fingers her face went slack-jawed.

"Webb."

"Let's go."

"How did you—"

"Later. Let's go."

She stood and let him take her by the hand. When they came through the curtain the barman was out from behind his roost and looking curious at the hallway. The two day drinkers were at a table now watching the action.

"The fuck is going on mister?" the barman asked.

"None of your concern."

"This is my place so it damn well is my concern."

Webb tugged Joni along to the bar, went around the far side and grabbed up the length of pipe he'd missed out on earlier. He swapped the broken bottle neck for it and brought it down hard on the bar top where it cracked like a gun shot.

"Me and Dan had business and now that business is done. You got any concerns beyond that, take it up with him."

The barman looked beyond the curtain. "Big Dan's back there?"

"He's taking a dip in the lake. Now we got to go."

Webb dragged the pipe along the back wall, smashing through bottles of whiskey, vodka and gin. The barman put his hands to the sides of his head as if the smashing glass hurt him physically.

Webb dragged Joni out of there fast.

In the Eliminator he tossed the pipe in the hollow back seat where it clanged to the bare floor. Joni put her seatbelt on and said, "How did you find me?"

"You didn't make it easy."

"Jesus Christ, Webb, I'm glad to see you."

"Goddamn stupid thing you did."

"I know, I know."

Gravel spit from under the tires as Webb tore the Eliminator out of the lot. His dad was right: being behind the wheel set everything right. He had control again. He felt at home.

"What the hell did you say to Big Dan to get me away from there?"

"I killed him."

Webb let that one sit in the air between them as he guided the car back onto asphalt. The tires hummed and he gave her more gas, turned on the headlights which flipped up out of their hiding place on the front grille.

"You killed Big Dan?"

"Yeah, and I don't think I'm done yet. Can you find your way back to the high roller you were with earlier?"

"Huh?"

"Your trick from earlier. Do you know where Dan took you?"

"I...I guess so. There was a church on the corner. I remember that."

"Of course there was."

21

The phone receiver felt like a gun in his hand, black and heavy. Calvin turned the rotor and spun the seven numbers of Vic's phone line.

"That thing we talked about? I'm in."

"Well, all right," Vic said. "Glad you came around. Not that you had much choice in it."

"When do you want to do it?"

"No time like the present." He sniffed sharply. "I'll be up for a while and she's in. She's retired to the guest room. Had a bit of a fight, y'see? First floor. Back left corner."

Calvin thought he'd have more time to prepare, then figured it was better not to think about it too long and get it over with. "Fine. Give me a half hour. And after I want to talk about what we're gonna do about Cantrell."

"One thing at a time, *amigo*." Vic hung up.

Calvin left Dorothy in bed with a book.

"You sure you'll be okay without me?"

"I got my watchdog." Dorothy patted the gun resting on her bedside table.

"I'm gonna bring an end to this," he said.

"I know you will."

They kissed and Calvin went to go get someone murdered.

He drove uncharacteristically slow. Made full stops at every sign and light. Thought hard with the radio off and the windows rolled up. By the time he pulled in front of Vic's house, he'd run down how he wanted it to go.

Vic would owe him. He might not see it that way, but Calvin could make him understand if it came to it. And Nancy, he might not wait for Vic to come in and play the jilted husband routine. He might just kill her as soon as he saw her for coming to his house and trying to poison his marriage. Not poison—venom. What snakes use.

Calvin went to the back corner of the house. He tossed pebbles at the window. He felt like a high school kid come to woo a girl. A light came on. Nancy peered out from behind the curtains. She saw Calvin and stiffened. She cracked the window, wrapping her thin nightgown around her.

"You win," he said.

She gave him a quizzical look.

"My wife thinks we're fucking," Calvin said with a shrug. "I figure we might as well be."

Her body softened. She watched him, looking for signs of a lie. With a quick glance over her shoulder she opened the window fully. "Come inside."

Calvin wasn't as graceful as he'd been in his younger days, but he got inside and tried to tamp down the anger building in his throat.

"It was a shit-all stupid thing to do, coming to my house," he said. "But damned if it didn't work out the way you intended. She thinks I'm a shit; alley catting around on her."

"You have to admit," she said with a sneaky pride, "it was

pretty clever of me."

Calvin knew he didn't have to hide any contempt. She'd expect it and a part of her needed it for the thrill of victory over him. If he gave in too easily, red flags would go up.

"Yeah, you got me good. I'm left with no other play."

Nancy let the nightgown fall open, revealing a lace set of undergarments from Paris, but bought in Des Moines. "Is it so bad?"

"I guess not. Like I said, if I'm gonna be accused of being bad, I might as well be bad."

Calvin didn't know how long he'd have to keep up the act before Vic came in to play the heroic and betrayed husband. It didn't have to be perfect, their little act. Just enough to get the look of shock on her face so any judge could see exactly what was going on.

"Let me show you how bad I can be," she said and slid backward onto the bed, slipping the nightgown off as she went. Calvin followed, annoyed that he was becoming genuinely aroused. She was a damn good-looking woman, if you didn't stop to think about all the other musclemen and bodyguards and pool boys who'd been there before. And if he didn't think about her standing on his front porch telling bold faced lies to his wife in order to hurt him.

She pulled him down on top of her and they began kissing. Calvin pictured Vic busting in any moment and didn't want to be covering her completely in the photo so he did a spin and turned her over so she was on top of him. She smiled and seemed to like him taking charge a bit, but still—ending up with her on top put her in the driver's seat.

She reached down and started undoing his belt.

"I bet you can fuck me in ways Vic never could," she said.

"He's got so much coke running through him he couldn't get his dick hard with a bicycle pump." She crushed Calvin's face with a violent, open-mouthed kiss.

"Maybe don't talk about Vic at a time like this," he said.

"Why not? The bastard has it coming. When you're sticking it to me, you're really sticking it to him."

"You sure know how to sweet talk a guy," Calvin said.

She unclasped her bra and tossed it aside. Calvin couldn't look away.

"You know the last one I fucked?" she said. "His coke dealer from Omaha." She slid off and nearly tore her panties while stripping them off.

"Wait, Omaha?" Calvin started to sit up on his elbows, but Nancy climbed back on top and reached for the button on his pants.

"Yeah. Omaha. He can't even get it from the company stash because Hugh is such a tight-ass he won't deal in the stuff."

"Vic gets his coke from Cantrell?"

"I don't know who, but whoever it was gave me a lame lay. Not like you're gonna do, right McGraw?" Her hand touched him, the first woman besides Dorothy in twenty years. "There he is."

"Hold on..."

Nancy slid down until her mouth hovered over his crotch as she took down his pants. With her out of the way Calvin could see Vic standing by the foot of the bed. He'd slipped in unnoticed and now looked down at them with pupils dilated as wide as the double barrels on the shotgun he held. No camera in sight. Calvin rolled off the bed. Both barrels exploded before he even hit the ground.

Nancy jerked forward, her face smashing into the

headboard of the bed. Her back was peppered with shot pellets, hundreds of tears in her flesh from her waist to the back of her neck. She stayed where she landed, head tilted against the headboard, arms out in opposite angles.

Calvin heard the stock of the shotgun crack open and two spent shells hit the floor. He pulled on his pants and stood, unable to avoid looking at Nancy's bloody body.

Calvin wondered if this had been his plan all along.

"A little pillow talk, huh?" Vic said. He drew two new shells from his breast pocket. Red cylinders on top of brass backings.

"How much did you hear?"

"Question is, McGraw." Vic dropped in one shell. "How much did you hear?" Vic dropped in the second and snapped the stock into place.

"Vic, for fuck's sake, are you working with Cantrell?" Be direct. No bullshitting. Life's too short.

"My brother is shortsighted. Ten years from now, shit, *five* years from now, coke is gonna be as popular as coffee in the morning. Gets you going to start your day. We could make millions."

Calvin looked around but had nothing to protect himself more substantial than a feather pillow. "They went after your dad."

"They weren't supposed to hurt him. *You* fucked that up."

Vic lifted the gun. Calvin hit the floor again and dove under the bed. Vic fired one barrel and tore apart the sheets on the bed, but missed Calvin. He scrambled in a desperate crawl under the bed and reached the other side where a fallen pillow blocked his view. He'd be coming out blind if he decided to stand, and if he stayed he was dead for sure.

He heard Vic's feet shuffling around the bed. They got

closer and he could see slight movement in the gaps between the bedpost and the pillowcase. He slid part way out, grabbed the pillow in both hands. Never had two weapons been more mismatched, but Calvin knew it was the man behind the weapon who would make all the difference.

As Vic turned the corner of the bed, Calvin pushed out on his back and flung the pillow up into the shotgun barrel, tilting it toward the ceiling. The second barrel fired and the plaster was pockmarked by pellets. Calvin slid the rest of the way out and got to his knees before swinging the pillow again. He clipped Vic's knees and knocked one leg into the other, pushing Vic off balance and forcing him to flail his arms to avoid falling to the floor. Calvin got to his feet. The feathers in his pillow were gathering in one end as he held a white-knuckled grip on the pillowcase. He swung the pillow at Vic's head. It pounded him with a soft sound, but jerked his neck to the side hard enough to stun him. Calvin quickly brought the pillow back across and snapped Vic's head the other direction. He didn't have time to reload, didn't have time to use the shotgun as a club.

Convinced he had used every last feather of usefulness in the pillow, Calvin dropped it and wrapped Vic in a bear hug. Vic pitched forward with a yell from deep inside and they fell back onto the bed. Calvin hit back to back with Nancy's dead body. He slid off on a coating of blood, dragging Vic with him and the shotgun still pinned between them.

They rolled next to Nancy in the bed. She remained still as if she was sleeping. Vic and Calvin grappled and twisted, Cal not willing to let go of his grip. They rolled over on Nancy's outstretched arm and the weight of them together snapped her elbow the opposite way. Calvin heard the crack and felt sick. He reared his head back and head-butted Vic. A cut opened up between Vic's eyes. Calvin did it again, this time to his nose.

Floodgates opened. Whatever damage Vic had already done to his sinuses all broke free at once in a torrent of blood like someone pulled a cork. Seeing Vic's stunned reaction to his own blood flow, Calvin unleashed him and snatched the shotgun away. He scrambled back off the bed, sliding to the floor, coated in blood from Nancy and darker, more viscous blood from Vic's nose.

Calvin stood on wobbly legs and held the gun like a baseball bat.

"You fuckin' traitor. Stand up."

Vic held both hands to his nose and screamed. Calvin knew he wouldn't be listening to any instructions. He grabbed Vic by the arm and dragged him off the bed. Nancy's arm was bent the wrong way, her back was coated entirely in red, her neck was bent so her eyes were on the ceiling, her skull nearly touching between her shoulder blades.

Calvin tugged Vic toward the door.

"Come on."

22

Webb knocked on the door using the pipe. He held Joni tight by the wrist. She wasn't getting away again. Sweat oozed from his pores. He pushed hair off his forehead, the pipe in his hand making the job unwieldy. He scratched at his chin and the whiskers there. Three days now and no shave. His dad wouldn't approve. He'd let Webb grow his hair a half inch longer than he thought it should be, but that was all the ground Calvin was likely to give before he started in on his son for being one of those, "Goddamn hippie types."

Joni stood behind him. "Webb, what are you gonna do?"

He kept his eyes on the door. "Don't you want me to fuck this guy up after what he did to you?"

"No. It's not like—" Joni stopped herself. It was too much to explain and she wasn't sure Webb would get it. She saw he clearly didn't know the role of women in the lowlife. A life she was born into and was stuck in like quicksand.

Webb understood more than she knew. *It's not like he didn't pay for it. It's not like she hadn't done it before. It's not like he beat me up.* Even if she kept to those low standards, he didn't have to.

The door opened and a short man with a balding head stood there with a cigarette in one hand. "What the hell is this?"

Webb hit him with the pipe across the chest. He fell back, dropping the smoke and coughing out what he had trapped in his lungs. Webb let Joni's arm go and followed him in.

"You wanna fuck young girls, is that it?" He hit him again across his stomach. "You ever ask if they want to be fucked by you, huh?" He raised the pipe to strike again.

"Webb, stop," Joni screeched.

He paused, holding the pipe high and ready to bring it down on his head this time. The balding man writhed and clutched at his gut. He choked out short, weak sounds of pain.

"Let's just go," Joni said.

Webb knew he didn't want to kill the man. Once was enough. He'd killed Big Dan. It ran through his mind again. He'd been blind with anger and here he was again behind a black curtain, ready to strike another man.

He took a step back, lowered the pipe, then reared back and kicked the man in the balls.

"Big Dan is out of business. Trying jerking off next time." They left him with the door open.

Inside the car, Webb threw the pipe into the back. He put his head in his hands and rubbed at his eyes with the heels of his hands until he saw sparkles of color flashing against the black.

"I'm sorry I ran out on you," Joni said. She timidly set a hand on his shoulder. "I got what I deserved."

Webb began to weep. For what he'd done and for what would make her say she deserved any of this.

"I wanted to rescue you."

"And you did." She rubbed his back, trying to calm him down. His words came out through choking sobs.

"I didn't want you to get hurt. I knew you would get hurt out there."

"It's okay. You saved me. I really couldn't believe it when you came through that door."

"I was too late."

"It's never too late. If I thought like that I'd have given up when I was ten."

There was so much in that one admission from her that Webb stopped his crying. She'd been through more. She'd been lower than him, made to feel worse, betrayed by people she loved. And then here he was, saving her from one fate and bringing her to the same fate with a fancier address.

The Ozarks or Iowa, a cadillac or a pickup truck—it didn't matter. She was property either way.

"I'm not taking you back," he said.

Joni stayed quiet.

"We can get you out. Get you somewhere. You don't have to go back."

"They'll kill you for that."

"No, they won't. My family has known the Stanleys since before they made a dime. They wouldn't have made shit without us around. They'll smack my ass, but they'll get over it."

"I can't let you do that."

"You have to." He looked at her with red eyes. "I was too late. I didn't do the job right in the first place." He looked down at the steering wheel. "I got out of the car."

"It won't last long, I'm telling you. Guys like Hugh, they get bored easy. A new girl will come along and I'll get tossed to the street."

Webb cranked the engine to life. "I'll call my dad. He'll

know what to do."

"Hey," she said. He turned to her. "Thank you. For real."
She leaned over and kissed his cheek. "What you did was
really groovy."

He put the car in gear. "I was too late."

Calvin pounded on the door with his fist.

"Hugh? It's McGraw. Open the goddamn door."

He pounded again. Vic wobbled on his feet next to Calvin,
his arm pinned behind his back in a vicious chicken wing arm
hold Calvin hadn't let go since they walked out of the guest
room in his house next door. The blood from Vic's nose had
already started to dry making a dark crust from his upper lip
down over the width of his chin and onto his neck and then
soaking far down his shirt.

The door flew open. Hugh stood there behind two
bodyguards. Calvin pushed past them.

"You got a rat problem, Hugh."

He shoved Hugh's little brother at him and continued on
into the house.

"McGraw!" Hugh called after him. "What the hell is going
on here?"

"Ask him, the dirty son of a bitch."

"I'm asking you. McGraw." Hugh stood in his shirtsleeves,
untucked and in only stocking feet. "I thought I heard shots."

"You did. Nancy's dead." Cal moved into the living room.
Hugh followed.

"How?"

"Vic shot her. He set her up, with my help I'm sorry to say."

"Set her up? Cal, put it in reverse here. Explain."

"Vic wanted her gone for all the catting around she's been

doing." Hugh didn't look surprised by the news. "She'd been after me as her next conquest so Vic had me fake like I was there to get it on with her and then he was supposed to come busting in and take some photos for the judge to see. Instead he comes in with a shotgun blazing away."

"The goddamn fool."

"Then he starts taking shots at *me*." Calvin hadn't sat. He stalked the room, flailing his arms as he spoke.

"Calm down, Cal. Why was he shooting at you?"

"Because of what she said before he shot her." Cal stopped still and fixed an eye on Hugh. "Vic is your mole working for Cantrell."

Hugh turned to see Vic being led into the room by the two bodyguards. Vic looked more than battered. He looked ashamed. Hugh put some pieces together in his mind.

"The goddamn coke."

"That's how they paid him," Calvin said.

Hugh approached Vic who cowered away from his big brother. "Is this true, Vic?"

Vic didn't answer, only started sobbing quietly, the tears making the blood run again in thin streaks off the bottom of his chin. Hugh looked down at his socks where droplets of his brother's blood splashed.

"Get him out of my sight," he told his men. They took him away to be dealt with later.

"Come to my office," he said to Calvin.

Hugh went straight for the bar once they entered his dimly lit office space. He poured them both drinks without asking. Calvin took the hard liquor. He needed something stronger than a beer.

"I'm goddamn sorry, McGraw. He shouldn't have dragged

164

you into it."

"I shouldn't have let myself get dragged." They each took a slug of the booze.

"Nancy's definitely dead?"

"As definite as you can get."

Hugh refilled his tumbler, but Calvin waved off a second round.

"And I'm damn grateful for what you did for pop," Hugh said.

But Calvin wasn't there for a pep talk. "I wanna know what the hell we're doing about Cantrell."

"Well, now that we've smoked out the mole...I guess we can start to put this thing behind us."

"Bullshit," Calvin said. "They came after my wife. They came after your father for fuck's sake. Ain't you gonna do something about it?"

Hugh went and sat behind his desk, reclining his swivel chair and swirling the bourbon in his glass. "I didn't know about Dorothy. I'm damn sorry about that. But this has larger implications, Cal. Whatever move we make has ripple effects."

Calvin set his drink down on the corner of Hugh's desk. "You seem sorry about a lot of shit tonight. Sorry don't get us shit, though. Just because Vic stops feeding him info doesn't mean Cantrell's done. He's got a taste now. He knows he can make some progress and he knows you won't move coke or heroin in Iowa. Like I said, you got a rodent problem and you're leaving a hole in the fence."

"I move hard drugs."

"I'm talking volume, Hugh. Cantrell's got cash coming out his ears because he's got the market locked up. Like it or not. Money means power and he wants more. You ever met

165

anyone who has either and didn't want more of both?"

Hugh studied the bottom of his drink. "What do you suggest we do?"

"He couldn't have struck more close to the heart than with Dorothy and Edmond. We gotta strike back at his heart. He's gotta go."

"I suppose I could ask Kirby to—"

"Where's your goddamn fight, Hugh? Where's your balls?"

Hugh set the drink down hard, bourbon splashing over the side.

"It's not that easy, dammit. We keep this up and people die. Business gets eroded. Supplies get interrupted. Ripple effects, McGraw. Business shit you don't have time for because you're too busy racing around behind the wheel of a car. What we have here is the start of a truce. Both sides retreat. We don't need to start a full on war."

"I'm not looking to start a war. I mean to end one."

Hugh held his stare. The two men with so much history between them.

"Dammit, Cal, I'm out of ideas here."

"I'm not," Calvin said. "I want to talk to the Greek."

Hugh waved his hand in front of his face like he was trying to erase the words from the air. "No, no, no. We don't need to go that far."

"Hugh, we can get to him, to Cantrell. I can't alone, but you can. Set a meeting – one on one. I just need to talk to the Greek and get him to make me something special."

Hugh set one fist inside the other and pressed them to his chin, thinking. The Greek was Nico Keropolis, an army buddy of Ennis Stanley, Hugh's brother killed in Vietnam. The Greek's specialty had been explosives. After he came back and settled in Cedar Rapids, he rarely came out of his garage where he'd tinker with bombs the way some guys loved a model train set. He never did anything with them. Not until the Stanley's came calling.

The Greek was only too happy to oblige them. He'd missed the explosions, the charge of seeing earth thrown to the sky, the ringing in his ears after a blast. The blood of his enemies.

When Hugh went to meet with him personally to secure a one-time job for a particularly stubborn owner of a movie theater who refused to pay protection, the Greek spent nearly a half hour showing Hugh photos he's taken in the jungles of Vietnam displaying his handiwork. And the best way to show the effectiveness of a bomb is to show the aftermath.

Nico had photos of body parts lying in charred craters, of limbs hanging from trees by shredded bits of skin, of bodies too mutilated to tell if they were man or woman, young or old. He showed Hugh this slide show with glee and total recall of every detail of the day. He'd tell you the weather, the sound of the insects in the trees, the smell of the smoldering blast site based on what accelerant he'd used.

Hugh left feeling nauseous and with a promise for Nico to hit the theater only when he was sure nobody was inside.

The job went off without a hitch and the Greek became legend. They used him twice more for smaller pipe bombs that were placed under cars and set off late at night while the vehicles sat in driveways. Nico had always seemed a little let down when he learned his work wouldn't mean any blood.

Calvin had devised a plan and he needed one of the Greeks devices to do it.

"You sure you want to go that way?" Hugh asked.

"I'm all ears if you got something else," Calvin said. "But I don't see any ideas coming from you and I'm tired of waiting. They broke into my house, Hugh. They held Dorothy at gunpoint. You better believe I will blow that fucker up for pulling shit like that."

Hugh exhaled and leaned back in his chair. "Kirby can take you. I ain't going back there."

"Do I really have to take Kirby?"

"Those two have gotten real friendly, go figure. Birds of a feather I suppose. And the Greek don't like strangers coming to his door. Word is the whole place is booby trapped and that's one I'm inclined to believe."

"All right," Calvin said. "So Kirby takes me. We head out early tomorrow, let him know." Calvin turned for the door. He looked past the doors where Vic had been taken. "How are you gonna handle Vic?"

Hugh stood up, drained the last of his drink. "You're not the only one who won't let an indiscretion stand. And I know you don't think it right now, but my vengeance can get downright biblical when I want to."

Calvin nodded at Hugh, knowing what he had to do, and left the room.

23

Behind the pool was a small structure. A cabana they called it, like they were in Cuba, not Iowa. Hugh walked the stone path from the house to the cabana where Vic waited with his two escorts.

"You can go, boys," Hugh said.

"You sure Mr. Stanley?"

"He's my brother. I'm sure."

The two bodyguards reluctantly left the room, but waited outside within earshot.

Vic sat in a chair, his face a swollen mess. The amount of blood was impressive. He looked like he'd gone twelve rounds with Ali. With his hands tied behind his back. When Vic did his trademark sniff, it sounded like a clogged drain.

"Vic." Hugh stood over him. "Jesus Christ, Vic."

"You don't know," Vic said.

"What don't I know? Enlighten me."

Vic resumed his crying. "What it's like to be your baby brother."

"You've been crying over that baby brother shit since I got a bigger bike for Christmas. It's bullshit."

"You won't listen to me. You won't listen when I tell you."

"So you went to Cantrell? He listens to you?"

"Cocaine is the future, Hugh. And you don't want it."

"I want repeat customers. Not ones that die off on me. That means quality shit, not some backyard shed cook from a team of wetbacks working minimum wage."

"We're not talking about selling to junkies. We're selling to businessmen. Lawyers. Singers. Actors. People with money already, they don't gotta go steal it to pay for the shit. It's coming here whether you like it or not."

Hugh wiped a hand over his mouth. It made him uncomfortable to see all the blood on his brother, like it was crusting on his own chin.

"So okay. You convinced me. That don't change things. You fucking ratted."

"I brokered a business deal. They wanted to cut us in, but you said no."

Hugh loomed over Vic, his voice booming. "They went after Dad."

"They weren't gonna hurt him."

Hugh grabbed Vic's blood-soaked shirt. "You knew about it?"

"Jesus, Hugh, you don't understand."

"I know all I need to."

He made a meaty fist and slammed it into Vic's nose, restarting the geyser of blood. Hugh pulled away, his knuckles aching. He reached onto a low table set in front of a rattan love seat. He took up a green marble ashtray and brought it back to Vic.

He stood over him, wondering what to say, but found nothing. He brought the ashtray down on Vic's nose. Smashing over and over at the one part of Vic that he knew was the source of the betrayal.

It didn't take many blows to cave in the front of Vic's face.

Hugh threw down the ashtray and it cracked the tile floor before skidding off under the love seat. The damnedable thing about it—he knew Vic was right. He'd been rethinking his position on harder drugs. He saw the writing on the wall. If the kid had a modicum of patience...but the drug didn't enhance that part of your personality. Quite the opposite.

So Vic would get what he wanted, he just wouldn't be around to see it.

Dorothy jumped when the phone rang. She had fooled herself into thinking she'd already gotten over the unsettling feeling of someone invading her home, but without the bourbon to steady her nerves even the most mundane household noises had her on edge.

She answered. "Hello."

"Mom, it's Webb. Is Dad there?"

"He's out right now, honey. When are you coming home? We're getting worried, Webb."

"Don't worry. There's nothing to worry about." His tone left Dorothy unconvinced. "I just really need to talk to Dad."

"Can I help you?"

"No...it's work stuff. I don't think you can."

Dorothy looked at the stained carpet, the blood nearly black now. She had moved the empty TV stand over it but the edges where the blood spread as it soaked into the fibers peeked out from underneath. "Webb McGraw, you might be surprised what your mom can handle."

"I don't know, Mom."

"When your dad has troubles, who do you think he comes

to?"

There was only static on the line for a minute. Then Webb explained. He told her the basics. Left out most of what happened to Joni. Left out him killing Big Dan and beating the other man. Left out them sleeping together.

"I don't think I want to bring her back, Mom. I don't think I can do that to her."

"Come home, Webb. Come here and we can figure it out together, but you're both much safer here." She knew there was more to Webb's story, but she held her own secrets so she didn't press him. She didn't feel confident that it really was any safer at home, but she wanted her boy back. She needed her family around her.

"There's a boat," Webb said. "It leaves from Burlington and heads downriver to New Orleans. I'm thinking of putting her on it."

Dorothy didn't want Joni going to Hugh Stanley any more than Webb did, but she also knew if he came home empty-handed he'd most likely be killed. Maybe the McGraw name would keep him from a shallow grave, but whatever he was in for it wasn't good and it wasn't anything she wanted for her son.

"Please just come home, Webb. The river and New Orleans will still be there if we can't figure something out."

More quiet. Dorothy could hear the far off mumbling of a diner or a truck stop. After a few seconds a recorded voice came on the line and told Webb to deposit twenty-five more cents to continue the call.

"I'm coming home, Mom. Hear me? I'm com—"

The line went dead, but Dorothy smiled and surprised herself when tears starting running down her cheeks.

24

Kirby insisted on sitting in the back seat, which annoyed Calvin to no end. He told him, "I'm not your fucking chauffeur." Kirby sat there anyway. And really, Calvin liked a little distance between him and Kirby. And with him in back, less chance of small talk.

Kirby had let himself slide a little more toward hippie. He hadn't shaved since Calvin saw him last and his scraggly beard seemed like it couldn't decide whether to stick around and grow or not. He wore a loose T-shirt and a leather vest, flared jeans and boots with heels.

"You got any tunes?"

"Just tell me where to turn."

"I will but it's like fifty miles, still. So do you have any tapes or what?"

"I might have something." Calvin leaned over and opened the glove box to find three cassettes: Merle Haggard, Bobbie Gentry and Johnny Cash. He tossed them over his shoulder to Kirby.

"What's this shit?"

"Music."

"We gotta get you turned on to something with a little

more style. You ever hear of the White Album? Creedence? Sly Stone?"

"I've heard of 'em. I like this."

They drove on in silence.

With nothing on the horizon but corn, Kirby told Calvin to turn off. The dirt road cut through a fallow field and up over a rise. Calvin felt like Custer riding into the unknown.

"He lives way out here?"

"For what the Greek does, he doesn't like prying eyes nearby."

Kirby sat up in the back and leaned over the seat to direct Calvin to a broken down farm house surrounded by rusted farm equipment. As Calvin searched for a place to park amid the derelict tillers and tractors and cultivators, he noticed the landscape around the house was pockmarked by holes. It looked like a field of land mines after a battle. Tiny eruptions of earth surrounded the house.

Cal checked the ground ahead of him as he walked to the door. He let Kirby knock. When the door opened with a haunted house creak, the Greek spread both his arms in welcome to Kirby and the stranger. Nico wore a camouflage jacket with his last name stitched above the breast. An olive drab headband held back long hair that hadn't seen a shower in a while. His gut protruded over his jeans and it took a belt and suspenders to keep them in place. He smiled and curled a patchy mustache that still showed skin through the coarse hairs. He certainly looked friendly and not like the mad bomber Calvin expected.

"Hey you old son of a bitch." Nico pulled Kirby into a hug. Calvin had never seen Kirby show true affection for anyone and even now he merely tolerated it, which was as sentimental as Kirby got. Nico clapped him on the back several times until Calvin knew he'd raised a welt. The Greek turned his attention to Calvin.

"You must be McGraw."

"Yep."

"Pleasure to know you." Nico put out a hand and Calvin took it only to have his own hand crushed in a vice grip. He pumped Calvin's hand like he was drilling for oil, then relented and let them inside. Kirby stood back, "After you," The grin on his face showed Calvin he knew what a character the Greek was. Calvin reluctantly stepped in.

The inside of the house was like a mad scientist's lab. Half completed experiments were in parts on every table. A ham radio with its guts open, a table with powders and fuses, a soldering iron unattended but curling a wisp of smoke from the red hot tip.

"So," Nico said. "You need to blow someone up?"

"He does," Kirby said. And with that he passed the conversation over to Calvin and went about poking at the various tables of fun around the house. Calvin knew a lot of the stuff was explosive so he didn't like Kirby touching everything like a toddler, but he needed what the Greek had to offer so he explained.

"I need something small and remote controlled."

"How small?"

"Something I can hide and get it right in the room with him."

"How powerful?"

"Strong enough to kill him," Calvin said.

Nico was treating this seriously, like a math problem to

solve. "Kill him from across the room? The next room over? Under his bed? What?"

"Same room. Hopefully right in his fucking lap."

"Okay, okay." Nico stroked his mustache while he considered it. "I can make it, but it's gonna be unstable. Like it can't get knocked around and shit, you know? Without something incendiary to light a fuse, I've got to think combustible combinations. Nitro and shit. But if they combine early it's... boom." He made a little explosion with his fingers and looked at the air in front of him like he'd just set off a firework on Fourth of July.

"Guess I'd better be careful then."

"Unless you think you can get some combustion going. Does this dude smoke cigars? I put a neat-o little device in a cigar once. Blew the guy's nose clean off his face. He lived though, and you don't want that. Although, man, living the rest of your life with no nose is pretty harsh."

"No, I want the whole funeral."

"Gotcha." Nico stood and looked around the room for the right table of supplies. "What's your delivery method? It's gotta be able to handle liquids."

He hadn't thought of it. "A bottle? Can you do a bottle?"

"Yeah, yeah. A bottle's perfect. Let me whip something up for you." He started gathering supplies. "So, were you in the shit?"

"Pardon me?"

"In 'Nam. Were you over there?"

"Oh. No, I wasn't."

"Let me tell you, those little gook fuckers can make explosives. Trip wires, land mines, you name it. Sneaky little fuckers too. They'd figure out a way to rig a bomb in your drawers so when you wake up to take a piss in the morning and pull your shorts down you blow your balls off."

The Greek's arms were full of supplies. "I gotta go out to the shed where I keep the nitro and shit. You wanna come?"

Calvin thought about what he said about it being unstable and declined the offer. "I'll stay here."

"Suit yourself."

"I'll go," Kirby said, looking up from a table with several hollowed out sticks of dynamite.

"Y'know what?" Calvin said. "I'll wait in the car."

"Gimmie about twenty," Nico said.

Calvin sat in the car devising the rest of his plan. He'd show up with Hugh and make a peace offering. They could do it with the Stanley family recipe corn liquor, an Iowa tradition since prohibition. He could sneak one of the bottles in the case and Trojan horse the bomb right inside.

He tried to think of what car to take. He felt like a woman staring at her closet before a first date. Had to be the right choice otherwise it could be a disaster. It had to be smooth so he didn't blow himself up, but Cal knew he could drive smooth in anything. Getaway power was a priority.

He wanted to check on Dorothy. He thought about asking to use the Greek's phone, but he didn't want to interrupt him in the middle of mixing a cocktail bomb. One slip of the wrist and they'd all go up.

Thirty minutes later Nico and Kirby came out the front door. The Greek held a bottle in front of him with delicate hands. To Calvin it looked like a normal bottle of clear booze, which was good. It would match the Stanley moonshine.

"Here you go, McGraw."

Calvin rolled his window down and reached for the bottle. Nico withdrew it.

"Be careful now, you hear?"

"I got it." He took the bottle by his fingertips. Up close he could see two different color liquids inside and the mechanism for dropping a little trap door and mixing the two chemicals. Calvin didn't know where in the car he could keep the bottle from getting jostled. Kirby would have to hold it, a prospect that didn't make Calvin feel great about the drive back, especially the dirt road they came in on.

"Looks like you're holding it, Kirby."

"Oh, no, I'm gonna hang out here for a few days. Let you guys handle your shit and have some fun blowing crap up around here."

Calvin held the bottle outside the window by the neck and from underneath.

"What do you mean you're staying here?"

"I mean you gotta drive back on your own." Kirby turned away and led Nico back to the house. "You got any of that grass around, man?"

"Hell, yeah. Let's toke." Nico turned, then spun back to Calvin. "Oh, you'll need this."

He held out the remote control which looked like a garage door opener. It even had a little clip he could use to hang it from his visor.

"Put it up there," Calvin said, gesturing with the bottle to the visor on the passenger side. He didn't want to set the bottle down for a second. Nico clipped it in place and then walked back to the house with Kirby.

Calvin didn't like having the bomb in the car with him. He liked even less the idea of Kirby and Nico getting stoned amid all the dangers out here, but he had to go anyway, and frankly, he'd rather not deal with Kirby for the drive so that part was good news. The bad news was that he had to carry the bomb bottle alone, and the best, softest, most secure place in the whole car to hold it was between his legs.

Calvin set the bottle down gently between his thighs and pushed them slightly together to cinch the bottle in place. He could absorb some bumps now, not knock the bottle over while taking a corner as long as he kept the side pressure on the bottle, and make sure the whole thing didn't tilt and mix the liquids prematurely.

If anything went wrong, of course, his balls would go first. But it was strong enough to kill Cantrell, it would kill Calvin too. He'd never have time to miss his balls. It was cold comfort to Calvin.

He exhaled once and turned the key. Suddenly the car sounded bigger, more vicious than ever. He turned the car around in a wide loop to avoid the farm equipment, and headed back down the dirt road at a respectable four miles an hour. He couldn't remember the last time he'd driven so slowly. He left his own driveway daily at fifteen at least. The speed was unbecoming a McGraw, but so was not having any testicles.

A deep rut swallowed the left front tire and the car tilted. Calvin sucked in and held a breath, slowed even more. A crow came down out of a nearby tree and landed on the hood, he was traveling so slow. The black bird felt like a bad omen and he honked the horn to get it to fly away which it did, but not before leaving a streaky white crap on his hood.

By the time he reached flat tarmac, he tasted sweat dripping into his mouth.

25

Calvin had never been more exhausted driving such a short distance in his life. When he pulled into his own driveway he nearly fainted from the release and the dehydration after he sweated out a good five pounds of body weight.

He gingerly lifted the bottle bomb, held it tight with the tips of his fingers and eased the car door open. He left his keys in the ignition, not wanting any more movement than was necessary. With short, shuffling steps he walked to the door and rang the bell.

He called, "It's me," to Dorothy, knowing she would be suspect of anyone coming to her door at night.

She answered and stayed behind the heavy door. He knew she would have the gun in hand in case it was a ruse, but when she saw he was alone she stepped out.

"Why are you ringing the bell?"

"Step back."

She did and he moved slowly into the house, thinking of where he could put the bomb down where it would be safe.

"Open the garage door," he told Dorothy. She did.

Calvin set the bottle bomb on his workbench next to an old carburetor and a ratchet set.

"Do I want to know what's in there?" she asked.

"Not really, no."

"You look a mess."

"I feel it. I need a shower."

"I'll fix you some supper."

Fifteen minutes later Calvin came downstairs feeling better. Dorothy cracked the top of a Pabst for him and he drank all of it without stopping. She knew her husband and had a second at the ready. He sat down and dug into the turkey sandwich she made him.

"Anything you want to tell me?" she asked.

"Only that it's going to be over tomorrow. Hugh and I are gonna go see Cantrell and work it out."

"Is that bottle an ice breaker then?"

"Sort of."

"I think I liked it better when you stayed behind the wheel."

"So do I."

A rumble sounded and the whirring of a chain drive. The garage door. Calvin went wide-eyed. He dropped his sandwich and ran for the garage. He yanked open the door to see Webb pulling the Eliminator into the garage. He held up both hands and yelled, "Stop."

Webb chirped the tires as he stopped the car. Calvin was lit up by the headlights, still chewing his food. The sweat had returned.

Once they got Webb redirected to the street, they invited him and Joni inside and made introductions. Calvin pulled Webb into a firm embrace.

"Good to see you, son. You had me a little nervous there. Kinda felt like I knew what it was like for those dads with their boys over in Vietnam."

"It was hardly that bad."

Calvin rubbed at a spot of blood on Webb's shirt. "You sure about that?"

"You know the Ozarks, Dad. If America has a war zone, that's it."

Dorothy laid a gentle hand on Joni's shoulder. "Can I get you anything to eat or drink?"

"I am kind of hungry."

"Well, sit, sit. I'll fix you up something right away."

Webb moved off toward the door. "I'm gonna get changed."

"Okay, hon. I'll have food set out for you both when you get back."

The rest of the night Joni was made to feel like an honored guest. Nobody asked any questions about how she came to be hunted by Webb or wanted by Hugh Stanley. No one asked what happened to them on their trip. Cal and Dorothy were too pleased to have their son home safe.

In return, Webb didn't ask about the stains on the carpet.

Dorothy made up the guest room for Joni. Webb felt confident she wouldn't try to run again and he wished her a good night. Asking her to sleep in his room was too soon.

Calvin got he and Webb both beers and they went to the back porch to talk.

"I don't know what to do, Dad. I can't take her back to Hugh."

"She seems real sweet. I mean it. The good news for you is that Hugh has bigger fish to fry right now so he won't be worried about her for a few more days yet. He hasn't asked about her once, in fact. The shit has hit the fan around here and it was a big cow pie. Made quite a mess."

"There's a boat to New Orleans—"

"Don't make any plans just yet. Let us take care of what we got to and then we'll talk to Hugh together, you and me. It'll work out."

"Thanks, Dad."

They both drank and listened to the cicadas in the trees.

"Appears you came out unscathed," Calvin said.

"I'm fine."

"That blood then?"

"Nobody who didn't deserve to lose it."

"Did you go the full McGraw on his ass?"

Webb grinned. "I suppose I did."

Calvin raised his beer in a toast. "That's my boy."

The next morning Calvin spent a half hour building a transport box for the bottle. He took an old milk crate and stuffed it with a pillow and blankets, then nestled the bottle down in the center and put more blankets on top. He felt he could drop it from the roof and it wouldn't smash.

He went to Webb, told him to take the day and relax. Try to get the dust of the road off him.

"Try not to worry," he said.

"What about Joni? What do I tell her?"

"Tell her not to worry either."

"I wish it were that simple."

"It's simple if you want it to be," Calvin said. "You try to think about how an engine works and it's damn complicated. But when it comes down to it you got five gears and that's all that matters. Think a little more on it and really you got forward and reverse. Two choices in life. Any situation calls for one or the other. You just gotta decide which is best for the situation you're in."

"Sounds like for now I'd be best off in park."

"There you go. Proved my point. You found the right choice for you."

He left Webb and got Dorothy from the kitchen where she was making Joni eggs and bacon.

"Pardon me but I need to borrow this pretty lady," he said.

"Of course," Joni said. "I'll keep an eye on the eggs, but I'll probably burn them. I can't cook worth shit." She blushed. "Sorry. Worth a darn."

"Don't you worry. I'll teach you all about eggs in a minute. You'll know more about 'em than a chicken."

Calvin and Dorothy stepped onto the front porch. He held her close.

"I'll be home late. Gotta go all the way to Omaha and back."

"You just make sure you *come* back."

"I'm going to stay in the car where I belong." He didn't mention that he would have his finger on the remote that would set off the bomb.

"I gotta say," he looked her in the eye. "It's kinda nice to be driving with a purpose. Strange as it is."

"You mean instead of going around and around in a circle on a race track?"

"I mean instead of sitting and watching other guys I taught to go around in a circle."

"You were just born an outlaw, weren't you?"

"Guess I was. Came out of the womb with a black hat on."

"No. Black hats are for the bad guys. You came out with a

tin star. It's just a little tarnished is all."

She pushed up on her toes and kissed him.

Calvin started his drive as if he were going to church with his grandma in the back seat. When it became clear his box worked to keep the bottle safe from knocking around, he drove more like normal. He pulled in front of Hugh's and got out, sure to shut the door gently.

He found Hugh in his office, still wearing the clothes he had on the night before. An empty bottle of bourbon was tipped on its side atop the desk. A half full bottle of whiskey sat at his elbow and his glass was begging for more.

The air in the room was stale and sour, the curtains drawn. Hugh slumped in his chair, hair askew. Calvin didn't think he'd ever seen the man with stubble on his chin. He looked up at Calvin like maybe he'd been asleep, but his bloodshot eyes read no sleep, the veins shooting out in jagged red lines like he'd been up for days driving crooked roads.

"Hugh? You okay?"

"It's taken care of." His voice was gravel. He raised the empty glass in a hopeless toast.

Cal could see it etched in his face. Vic. He didn't know if Hugh would have the stomach for it last night, but now he knew. He had the look of a man who didn't just witness the act performed by one of his flunkies. Hugh was damaged the way only a man who killed his own brother could be.

Calvin leaned over and flicked on the desk lamp, trying to cut through the murkiness of the office. The light lit up tiny dots of red on Hugh's shirt. Blood. Not his own.

"What about Cantrell? We were supposed to go see him."

"I'll be fine." Hugh swiveled his chair and made like he

wanted to stand up. Gravity had other plans. He raised up a few inches, then crashed back in his seat. Calvin stepped forward. The ice bucket on the edge of the desk was filled with only water.

Calvin could hear the fine hum of the stereo and saw that it was on, but the record on the turntable had run out and the needle spun on an endless loop as the grooves looped forever inward toward the label but never reached their destination. He lifted the arm and switched off the turntable. A jazz record. John Coltrane. Hugh was about the only one he knew who listened to that freaky shit. Calmed him, he said.

"Hugh, I'm all set to go see Cantrell. I'm not waiting."

"You saw the Greek?"

Calvin nodded.

Hugh slurred, "You gonna shove it right up his ass?"

"I kinda needed you to get me in the door. If it's a high level meet, we could get inside. Just me is gonna be tougher."

"Ain't tougher than nothing I've done." Hugh's eyes settled down in his lap. Calvin could see a wash of sadness come over him. He reached for the whiskey bottle. Calvin stepped forward to move it out of his reach. He saw behind the desk where a pool of vomit soaked into the rug—the sour smell explained.

"I think you've had enough," Calvin said.

"You're right." Hugh sat back in his chair and closed his eyes.

Calvin needed a new plan, or at least a new take on his old one. One thing he knew he needed was the peace offering.

"Hugh, hold on before you pass out. I need a case of that Stanley corn liquor. Where can I get one?"

"Liquor?"

"The Stanley mash. Where is it?"

Hugh looked around the room, confused. "Basement. Got some there." He sat back again and shut his eyes.

"Thanks, Hugh. You sleep it off. I'll get this taken care of."

"I took care of it," Hugh mumbled again.

"I know you did." Calvin turned for the door.

"Tell me I did good."

Cal stopped. He could hear Hugh on the verge of tears. He didn't turn to face him. Couldn't bear to see him cry, especially since Calvin had delivered Vic to his death.

"He was a rat, Hugh. You did what you had to."

Calvin left the room.

26

The case of Stanley corn mash sat in the trunk as Calvin drove back home. He needed backup. Someone to stay with the car. Webb was back on the job sooner than he planned.

Calvin outlined the plan, showed him the remote, the bottle. He told Webb about the men who came to their house and who Dorothy killed.

"That is...damn." Webb felt his skin get hot. He wanted to strike back at Cantrell too. "What do you need?"

"A driver. No, better, I need a McGraw."

"I'll do it."

Calvin followed his ritual with Dorothy. They never said goodbye when he went on a job. It implied he might not come back. For Calvin, driving into danger was same as a trip to the store for milk. Dorothy clung to him a little longer though, hoping he wouldn't notice.

Joni kissed Webb softly on the lips.

"Be safe, okay?"

"Yeah. You too."

"I'll be fine here with your mama to protect me."

They both smiled. Joni untied a red bandana she'd had knotted around the strap of her bag since she didn't know when. It went with her everywhere, and now she wanted it to go with Webb. She tied it around his neck, leaving it loose. She reconsidered and slid it up and around his forehead, pushing back his shaggy hair.

"There. Your suit of armor."

"Thanks."

She kissed him again. He didn't know what to do with his hands.

When Webb came outside to get in the car, Calvin looked at the new bandana and made a sour face. Webb knew there was little else worse than if he'd turned into, as Calvin put it, one of those goddamn flower people. Webb didn't even love the headband, but he intended to keep it there.

"She gave it to me."

Calvin nodded. He handed Webb the remote device. "You ready for this?"

"Yes, sir."

"I have no idea how things will go inside, but I ain't sitting around here waiting for them to try again. I'm bringing the fight to them. Driving forward, not reverse."

"What happens when we blow it?"

"We get out fast."

Webb turned the remote over in his hand. "How much reach does this thing have?"

"Not much. We'll need to hit it when we're still in the driveway."

"And then get the hell out of Dodge."

"Exactly."

Webb shook his head. "Wish we had a goddamn race car or something."

189

Calvin smiled, light coming to his eyes. "Son, you've given me an idea."

Marshall Pruitt shook Calvin's hand like a piston in top gear.

"Good to see you, Cal. Good to see you. And who's this then?"

"That's my son, Webb."

Pruitt let go of Calvin's hand and took up Webb's, pumped it for all it was worth. "Two McGraws. I'll be damned."

"I'm here to ask a favor, Marshall," Calvin said. "One that will help me make my decision."

"Sure, sure, sure. Whatcha need?"

"I need a car." Pruitt's face twitched slightly, but his permanent grin didn't falter. "I want to get to know the equipment better. I want to see what you're playing with here. To find out if I'm truly qualified."

"Oh, we know you're qualified, Cal. But you want a vehicle—you got one."

Pruitt leaned out his office door and shouted, "Get Dylan up here. Tell him to bring the keys to number thirty-four."

"I really appreciate this, Marshall."

"Not at all, not at all. I think after you experience one of our superior vehicles, you won't be able to resist coming to join the Empire Racing family."

Pruitt clapped Calvin on the shoulder and gave a toothy grin to Webb.

"I'm sure you're right," Calvin said. "That whole only-turn-left thing though, that's non-negotiable?"

Pruitt gave him an open mouth smile, thrilled that Calvin was joking with him.

"Good one, Cal. Sharp. You'll fit right in around here."

Calvin and Webb were strapped into a stock car painted in a lime green with blue stripes and wearing a bright white number thirty-four in big block print on the doors, hood and roof.

The doors were welded shut so they had to climb in through the window. The inside of the car was stripped. The two bucket seats were about all that remained. It was all Calvin needed.

Roll cage, chest harness straps, St. Christopher medal super glued to the dashboard. Calvin fired the engine. There would be no element of surprise in this noisy beast.

He stuck his hand out the window to thank Marshall who took it and hammered his elbow up and down like he was working a jack getting set to change a tire.

"I'll have her back by morning," Calvin said.

"You have a good ride, now, y'hear?" Marshall waved them off. "Remember now, Empire needs you."

Pruitt had told one of the office women to stand at the end of the parking lot with a green start flag. She waved it as they pulled out. When Calvin got onto street he turned and gunned the engine. The car leapt forward with a roar. He smiled as his body pressed against the seat, the G forces pushing him back. An impressive machine and maybe the thing that would save their ass when they needed a quick getaway.

He turned to Webb. "I'll be damned. These things do turn to the right."

Dorothy stood behind Joni as she stirred a pot of chili made with Dorothy's secret recipe.

"So, you and Webb became awful close out there on the

road."

Joni blushed. "Yes, ma'am. Quite close."

"He seem like husband material to you?"

"Well...I...I mean—"

Dorothy waved the question away. "Too soon. Sorry about that. It's just, sometimes you know. Can't say how, but you just know."

Joni stopped stirring and thought back.

"It sure wasn't when he first showed up." She backtracked so she didn't offend. "Not that he's not cute and all. But there were no sparks."

"You need sparks to start an engine." Dorothy had picked up on several of Calvin's sayings over the years. Sometimes they surprised her.

"But the second time..." Joni thought about when Webb came crashing through the door at the Royal Club. "That time was different."

Dorothy smiled. "I know what you mean." She turned her attention back to the chili. "Keep stirring now. It's got to simmer a good long time."

They had the extra bottle of moonshine wedged between a roll bar and the bodywork of the stock car, neck down so it wouldn't slide around the sparse interior of the race car. With the one bottle in the center of the case removed and substituted with the bottle bomb from the Greek, Calvin's plan was in place, but he didn't feel any too confident about it.

Urging the powerful engine down the stretch of four-lane highway relaxed him, though.

"So I told you what happened at our house," Calvin said to Webb. "You gonna tell me what went on out there while you were away?"

"I told you most of it," Webb said.

"Most isn't all."

Webb studied the corn fields out the window. "You'll tell me I screwed up."

"Seems like you already know that end of it."

"What do you want me to say, Dad? I fell for her, okay? I didn't plan it. Just happened."

"Who ever plans to fall for a girl?"

"I know it's dumb. She's Hugh's property. That's what bugs me even more about it."

"And that's why we never know too much about the cargo. You get there, you make the delivery, you go home."

"I know, Dad. I blew it. But I really don't know if I can deliver her right to his door, y'know?"

"I know. We'll figure something. One figuring at a time though."

"Speaking of," Webb leaned out the window a bit to take in the brightly colored paint job and the big block numbers on the side of the car. "Do you think maybe we're drawing a little too much attention in this thing?"

"It's a trade-off," Calvin said. "What she lacks in subtlety she makes up for in acceleration."

To prove his point, Calvin gunned the engine and the car moved from sixty to over eighty in a matter of seconds. Not long after they heard the telltale sound of sirens behind them.

"Sometimes," Calvin said, "it's like they want to be humiliated."

He waited until the State trooper was only two car lengths behind him before he settled down on the gas pedal again. The car took off with a roar. The cop sped up but his engine sounded more like an asthmatic on a treadmill.

Calvin threw a glance to the case of bottles in the back, but felt confident in his packing job. As long as he didn't flip it, he knew he'd be okay

"Hang on," he told Webb. Getting the attention of the cops was not a good thing on their way to this meeting, but he needed this. He needed the gasoline-in-his-veins feeling.

Calvin focused on the road and the traffic ahead of him. All other worries faded away as he zeroed in on the connection between him and the car. He could feel the road beneath him through the wheel, the seat. He could see what each car would do before they did it. He wove the stock car between the commuters and day drivers, the tourists and truckers. The trooper fell behind quickly.

Faced with cars in both lanes ahead of him, Calvin steered the car onto the soft shoulder. The tires bit at the loose gravel surface but he kept the speed up and tightened his grip on the wheel. He passed the obstruction while still doing ninety. A grin grew across his face.

The trooper's car spit dirt and grit as it followed, nearly fishtailing out but climbing back onto solid pavement before taking off after him again, though now farther back than before.

Calvin veered over and made for an exit. The trooper's car followed. Calvin aimed the car for the ramp, then pulled sharp to the left and the stock car slashed across the lane to rejoin the highway. For the trooper, it was too late. He turned, but slid sideways, mashing the EXIT sign as he went and sliding off into the gully between the highway and the corn.

Calvin let loose a victory whoop.

"Won't they have cops all over the state on the lookout for

us?" Webb asked.

"Nah. He won't call it in. Be too embarrassed. They never do. He'd have to explain what happened and then it's a lifetime of getting shit from the rest of their guys. No, we're good."

They passed a sign: Omaha 90 Miles. Calvin stayed happy the rest of the way.

27

It hadn't been easy to wrestle an address out of Hugh, but Calvin had more luck with his secretary. He told her to check in Vic's Rolodex, not Hugh's, and she came out with it in minutes.

The arrival of a stock car in the driveway caused a stir among the bodyguards and musclemen of Cantrell's. Calvin shut off the engine and heard it sigh with the sound of a job well done. He breathed deep.

"You got the remote?"

"Right here," Webb said, setting the device on the dashboard.

"If I'm not out in a half hour—you drive away and press that button."

"You'll be out."

"I hope so." Calvin extended a hand to his son. "I'm proud of you, son."

"Love you, Dad. See you in a few."

Calvin slid out of the window and helped Webb ease the case of liquor gently out, then Webb moved into the driver's seat and immediately put his hands at ten and two where Calvin knew they would stay.

Calvin carried the case in front of him and watched the skeptical crowd of Cantrell soldiers watch him approach.

"I come bearing gifts from Hugh Stanley."

He let the message get murmured through the crowd until one man left to go pass it on up the chain of command. Calvin stayed where he was, unthreatening. He couldn't remember the last time he'd been in Nebraska. Or any reason he would ever have to return. *It's like Iowa minus all the cosmopolitan excitement*, he thought. *And that's saying something. Nothing good, but something.*

A minute later he was waved inside. He swallowed hard and entered enemy territory.

Toby Cantrell sat in an office more rich in dark woods than Hugh's. There was a western theme to the decorating with paintings of horses thundering across the plains, a few sculptures of cowboys mid-rope and a pair of longhorns hanging on the wall behind his desk.

He did not get up when Calvin entered. The man who ushered him in stayed along with two other guards. They closed the door behind them and sealed Calvin in—four against one, with more outside.

"This..." Cantrell said, looking Calvin up and down, "...is unexpected."

"Mr. Stanley is hoping we can make amends and nobody else has to die." *Except you, fucker*, Calvin held back.

"And this is...?" Cantrell indicated the case.

"A peace offering." Calvin took a step toward the desk, but a hand on his shoulder stopped him. He was redirected to a short coffee table in front of a deep brown leather couch. He wanted to be closer, to make sure the bottle blew up the target, not just his furniture. He set the case down and his arms gave

197

thanks. He flexed his fingers a few times to stretch them. "Old family recipe corn liquor from the Stanley's personal stash."

Calvin went to open the box and again a hand stopped him. Cal couldn't even see the directions Cantrell was giving, if he was giving any at all. One of the men stepped over and flipped the box open. A grid of twelve bottle tops stared back at him. All Calvin could see was the one bottle different from the others and he hoped the man wouldn't pull that bottle or this meeting would be very short.

The man went for the bottle closest to him. Calvin could breathe again. The clear liquid inside appeared as water, but Calvin knew it was a hundred and eighty proof. The man brought the bottle to Cantrell for inspection. He turned the bottle over in his hands a few times. No label, only a thin wax seal over the cap.

"Why didn't Stanley come himself?"

"He wasn't sure how the gift would be received. Plus, he's grieving. You may have heard his father was assaulted the other day."

Cantrell gave a pursed lip look at Calvin, not appreciating the joke.

"Also," Calvin continued. "His brother Vic is dead."

Cal let that one sink in the palpable silence of the room.

"Vic, huh?"

"A little too much." Calvin tapped a finger to the side of his nose. He wasn't sure if Cantrell bought it or not.

"And so he sends you. A nobody."

"My name is Calvin McGraw. I'm somebody."

Cantrell smiled. "You're McGraw? The car makes sense now. My boys tell me you pulled up in something that looked like Richard Petty. Is that right?"

Calvin nodded.

"And so you're here to make peace with me."

"It would benefit the both of us."

"You're on my shit list, boy."

Calvin nodded again, tight lipped. Cantrell waited to see if he'd rattled Calvin. When the silence became too much he slapped a hand down on the desk and said, "Well, let's taste this here corn liquor."

He waved two fingers and glasses appeared at his side from one of his men. Cantrell twisted the top off the bottle and poured. He raised his glass, nodded for Calvin to come forward and take his.

"You first," Cantrell said. Cautious. And close to the truth. That case would be his undoing, but not by poison.

Calvin took a swig of the clear liquid. His eyes started burning from the fumes before a drop even touched his lips. The liquor lit up the inside of his mouth when it hit. He tried to choke it down as fast as he could to make the burning stop. He might not have been poisoned, but it sure looked like it.

Cantrell laughed and knocked back his drink in one. He took a pause, composed himself, then let out a holler. "I said god *damn*." He did not refill the glasses.

"Special recipe you say?"

"For special occasions."

"So what's the agreement?"

"You can have cocaine. Hugh doesn't want to touch it. You can have it in Iowa, but you leave the rest to us."

Cantrell contemplated. He studied Calvin for sincerity, seemed to see it in his watery eyes.

"And this killing bullshit ends. Full stop. Right now?"

"That's what we want."

Cantrell rose from his chair. He wore a heavy belt buckle with gold ropes around the edges, blue jeans, a turquoise ring on his pinky. He grinned as he came around the desk.

"Well, that's what we want too."

"So we have a deal?"

"I think we can work something out." He shook Calvin's hand. Cal hated to do it, could only picture the man giving an order to invade his home and have him killed, but he knew his justice would be served soon enough.

"Enjoy that special recipe," Calvin said.

"I will. On special occasions."

"I'll bring this news right back to Hugh. He'll be pleased."

"You do that." He clapped Calvin on the back. "And tell old Hugh not to be a stranger. Come up and see us some time."

"Thanks for your time."

Calvin left, taking a last look at where the case of bottles sat and where each man in the room was. If Cantrell stayed standing it would be ideal. If he rushed the case out of there and into a liquor cabinet or a pantry somewhere, disaster.

Cal tried to hustle down the hallway as quick as he could without making it look obvious. He needed Webb to hit that button.

When he got to the doorway he saw a crowd had gathered around the car. Men peered inside, ran their hands over the decals. But Webb was on the job. Hands on the wheel, eyes forward. Calvin gave a subtle nod and Webb sparked the car to life, then slid over to the passenger seat. The crowd of bodyguards stepped back and laughed at the absurdly loud rumble of the engine.

"Let me show you how you do it, boys," Calvin said. He

rushed forward and hopped up into the empty window, set his hands on the roof and slid his legs inside in one smooth motion. He landed in the drivers seat and took hold of the wheel. Beside him, Webb pressed the button. Two seconds later they all heard the blast.

28

Screeching tires filled the air as the sound of the explosion faded. A puff of smoke wafted out the open front door and mixed with the burning rubber smoke Calvin laid down on his way out. He didn't know the engine well enough yet, plus he was keyed up and over-excited so he popped the clutch too quickly and ended up with tire spin. Not a great start, but old number thirty-four gripped quickly and they shot out of there fast.

He hated driving away without knowing if the blast had worked, but Webb turned his head to the house as they drove away and saw a gaping hole in the back corner and flames licking out to reach the second floor.

"No way he survived."

"I damn well hope not."

Calvin ran through the escape route in his mind. One of his big rules: never enter a place you don't know the way out of. He turned left, confident they could be out of the neighborhood and nearly to the highway before any of Cantrell's soldiers could make it to a car and crank the engine. After that it was all up to the stock car to do the work.

The car's back end came around too far and Calvin had to

wrestle it back in line. He'd been pushing it on the highway, but not to its limit the way he was now. The massive engine was a different beast when he really gave it all she had to offer. Ahead of him he saw something he hadn't expected.

Two cars were t-boned into one another and spread out across the two lane road. The houses on either side sat behind a brick wall to the right and a six foot hedge on the left. He squealed the stock car to a halt.

The two drivers of the cars were out and inspecting the damage. Both men turned and stared with slack jaws at the race car now only feet from them.

"Heard a goddamn explosion," one explained. "Didn't know what the hell was going on."

"Are they having a race?" the other asked.

Calvin threw it in gear and peeled out the opposite direction.

"You know how to get there? Webb asked.

"Can't be too hard. Three rights make a left. We'll just make the block and be back on track."

The pickup on the finely tuned engine was impressive. He was up to sixty in a matter of five seconds and whizzing past Cantrell's driveway. As he passed, three cars banged out onto the street.

"Shit," Calvin said. This complicated things.

"Three of 'em," Webb said.

"I saw 'em."

The street took a gentle curve to the right and went on for a stretch without an intersection. With each turn like that he was more off the grid that could easily lead him back to the highway. Meandering subdivisions like this one were the rage in suburban design. Gone were the identical layouts designed on graph paper from the fifties. Now everyone wanted organic shapes, winding lanes, and cul-de-sacs. Calvin just wanted a way out of this maze.

He came to a four way stop and did a quick scan to his left, seeing no one. He let his foot off the gas for a second, downshifted, then accelerated through the turn without stopping. Let them keep up with that.

Behind them three sets of tires screamed against the pavement and the tight turn.

"That's one," Calvin said, counting the turns.

The new street—named after another goddamn tree— turned slightly south as it rolled over a gentle rise. A park showed up on his right where a street should be. He was getting farther away from his route to the highway. Deeper into Nebraska, a hell hole no man should have to sink into.

The first gunshot told him the men behind them were desperate. Nobody expected to hit anything at that range, unless they were snipers or idiots. Calvin didn't like the idea of them breaking out the guns next to a park, either.

"Looks like a main road over there," Webb said, pointing across the park where four lanes of traffic flowed in both directions.

Ahead, Calvin couldn't see the next turn off. The rolling green hills of the park went on and on. A swing set sat beside a pond which fed a small creek running off into a larger pond below. Probably a nice place to visit on a Saturday afternoon. Not today, though.

Calvin cut the wheel. The stock car had solid shocks, not built for banging over obstacles. When they went up and over the curb Calvin and Webb felt it in their spines. The tires spinning at seventy miles an hour bit into the soft grass, kicking up a tail of turf and mud behind them.

A young mother screamed and lifted her child out of a swing, but Calvin was headed the other direction, toward the small pond and the creek.

Webb turned to see all three of Cantrell's cars follow.

"They're on our ass."

"Stupid of them."

"What's that make us for doing it first?"

"Desperate."

The ground fell away in an easy slope Calvin guessed would be good for sledding in winter. The car took it well, but banged the front fender when the ground flattened out. Being high above the pond gave him a good vantage point for the best crossing. He spotted a section of bank beside the footbridge over the creek. There was enough of a rise there he felt sure he could make the four foot jump over water.

The back tires spun a little on the grass and he went into it without as much speed as he would have liked, but number thirty-four hit the bank on the upturn of land and the car left the ground for a second. Long enough to jump the creek.

Ahead of them, people scattered. One man fishing on the bank of the pond turned to watch them go by and fell in the water.

Cantrell's men followed in Calvin's tire marks. The first two cars made the jump with scrapes of metal when they landed. The third car took a bad angle and ran his car into the footbridge while in midair. The wood splintered and the car spun, landing sideways on the bank and tilting up before flopping over on its hood.

"One down," Webb said as he looked through the back window.

"Two to go," Calvin said.

He made the turn off the grass onto the main road. Cars around them spun and braked, gnarling traffic in both directions. Calvin turned right and upshifted now that the tires had grip again. After Calvin cleared a gap in the traffic, the two Cantrell cars easily made the turn onto the road and kept up the pursuit.

"I don't want them getting to the highway with us," Calvin said.

"No gun in the glovebox of this one."

Calvin took a quick look over his shoulder. There wasn't much of anything in the car. But he saw one thing.

"Take off that bandana."

"Now, Dad? Really?" Webb was annoyed his father's judgement of his appearance would crop up now of all times. "She gave it to me for luck."

"Take it off so we can use it."

He started to untie the bandana. "What for?"

"Grab that bottle of corn liquor."

Webb got the bandana undone, reached around for the bottle they had wedged in back.

"Soak it and stuff it in the neck," Calvin said.

Webb got it. Like a molotov cocktail. Sounded great, with one hitch. "What do we light it with?"

"Shit." Calvin looked around the car again, unable to take his eyes off the road for more than a split second. Traffic was not too heavy, but at his speed they passed cars fast on all sides. He looked behind them, saw the two cars in pursuit and did a little math. They were a good eight to ten car lengths behind. They'd keep coming, even if he could outrun them back to Iowa. Once they realized their top man was dead, the soldiers would retreat. Nobody in this business had enough sacrifice in them to go rogue and avenge Cantrell's death.

The men following him now though, they were either clueless about Cantrell or just caught up in the pursuit. He had to get them off his tail one way or another.

Calvin swerved right, jammed on the brakes. The stock car slid on smoking tires to an angle in front of a bus stop. Calvin pointed to a man in a business suit and briefcase standing and staring at them, shocked into stillness.

"Cigar," he said to Webb who leaned out the window and plucked the cigar from the man's mouth. The businessman stood in shock and watched it all go down, paralyzed. Webb put the cigar to the bandana soaked in hundred and eighty proof moonshine and watched it ignite. The small bus stop crowd scattered. A woman screamed. The businessman dropped his briefcase and ran.

Webb leaned farther out the window and turned to see the Cantrell soldier's cars approaching and also slam on their brakes.

Webb threw. The bottle smashed across the hood of the closest car. Fire spread over the car like a new paint job. He dropped the cigar and Calvin blasted number thirty-four out of there and through the next intersection.

Two men threw open doors and sprinted from the burning car. After a moment of reversing and repositioning, the third car fell in behind them.

Up ahead was a street name Calvin recognized. Another right turn here and he'd be on the way to the highway another nine miles down the road. A nine mile straight in which to somehow eliminate his final threat. He spun the wheel, cutting off a pickup truck who blasted his horn.

Cantrell's men followed. He knew they'd be as eager to

keep him from the highway as he was to reach it.

"Got any ideas?" he asked his son.

"Run him off the road."

"We get close enough to push him and he's got guns. Not a good combo."

"I don't know then."

A smell wafted through the car and with it came an idea. Ahead of them, also aiming for the highway, was a semi truck pulling a trailer full of beef. Unslaughtered cattle riding shoulder to shoulder and laying their stink in a cloud after them.

"We can't push them but we can push somebody else," Calvin said. He gunned the engine, weaving through traffic to pull side by side with the cattle truck. He watched behind him as he slowed to keep even with the truck. The Cantrell soldier car came up fast. When he was only a few car lengths back, Calvin cut the wheel and bumped the truck. He accelerated and got out in front of the truck, cutting him off close enough to clip his headlights. The truck swerved. Calvin followed him, sticking right on his nose and hoping the semi wouldn't roll right over the both of them. The truck driver kept trying to avoid a full on collision with Calvin and did exactly what Calvin wanted him to do—the truck jackknifed.

The cargo mooed and dropped patties of shit as the truck slid sideways across the four lanes. Cantrell's men had been coming up fast and couldn't stop in time, as Calvin expected. The car rammed into the trailer hauling the beef and the top sheared off the right side of the car.

Blood mixed with cow shit dripped from the trailer. The driver remained in his seat with his head attached, but the trailer began to tip. Calvin gunned number thirty-four out ahead of the tilting semi. He and Webb watched as the trailer filled with shifting and panicking cattle rolled onto its side, tearing a hole in the slatted side of the trailer and dumping confused and anxious cows onto the road.

When the trailed tipped, Cantrell's car broke free from the wedged-in crush and straightened out. The driver was dazed from the impact and showed little control over the car. A pair of cattle fell from the sky and landed on what was left of the roof.

The whole screeching, mooing, shitting mess came to a sliding halt in the street amid a chorus of horns and screams. Calvin parked the stock car.

"What are you doing?" Webb asked. "Let's go."

"I gotta know."

Cal slid out of the window and ran to the mangled heap of meat and metal that used to be Cantrell's car. He found the driver under a side of beef, the steer split open and leaking gore over the car and the man. Calvin had to shove aside a steakhouse worth of raw meat to get at the driver and when he did he grabbed the man's lapels which were slick with cow's blood.

"Is he dead?"

The driver was nearly dead himself. His head lolled and his eyes were unfocused. Calvin didn't know how much of the blood was his and what belonged to the steer.

"Is Cantrell dead?" Calvin insisted.

The driver peeled his eyes open long enough to see who was asking. "He's dead. You blew him up."

"Then this is over. You hear me? It's over."

Calvin let the man go. He knew the driver would probably never make it to deliver the message but with Cantrell gone, he knew it was over. For now.

In the chaos, Calvin went unnoticed. He returned to the car to find Webb had slid into the driver's seat, ready for a quick escape. Calvin sat in the shotgun seat.

"Get me out of this fucking state."

29

When they arrived home the two McGraw men were wrapped in hugs. Dorothy held Calvin tight and they didn't speak. Joni wrapped her arms around Webb's neck until he could barely breathe.

"Oh my God, I thought you might be dead."

"I'm okay. It's all right."

Calvin led Dorothy inside. "Let's give them their privacy."

Joni let his neck loose and kissed him. He needed air, but he didn't push her away and didn't want it to end.

She pulled back. "Y'know, when I split I didn't think anything of it, really." Joni wiped tears from her eyes. "But when you left...something just came over me, I mean, I didn't know how much I'd miss you."

"Yeah," Webb said. "Me too."

"Oh, you're gonna be one of those, huh?"

"One of what?"

"Those quiet types. I always gotta drag it out of you."

"I'm from Iowa."

Dorothy hugged him again.

"So what happens now?" she asked.

"I go talk to Hugh, see if he's heard anything. I think it's over, though."

"And them?" She nodded her head outside where Joni and Webb were still wrapped in each other's arms.

"That may be tougher." He cracked the top on a Pabst and drank deep.

An hour later Calvin and Webb were both showered and well fed. Both women wouldn't leave their sides.

"I'm gonna go talk to Hugh," Calvin announced.

Webb started to stand. "Let me get my jacket."

"No. You stay. I think the little lady missed you."

Dorothy crossed her arms in mock offense. "And what about me?"

"You know better."

Calvin lifted the keys to the stock car from the counter. "Gotta go return this first."

"He'll be expecting an answer."

"He'll get one."

Calvin and Dorothy traded a look. She knew his decision. He didn't even need to say it out loud. "Hurry back, outlaw."

Calvin pulled number thirty-four into the pit row at Empire racing. The car had seen better days, but the engine still hummed. A mechanic stared at the battered car as it rolled in.

Marshall jogged out to meet Calvin. He stopped short seeing the state of the car.

Calvin saw his face as he slid out the window.

"A little cow's blood. Washes right off."

Marshall stood dumbfounded.

"Thanks for the test drive. Mighty impressive vehicle you got there." He gave a nod to the mechanic. "But," he tossed the keys to Marshall who caught them in midair. "I'm afraid I won't be able to take the job, Marshall. I have to honor my true calling."

Marshall cocked his head like a confused dog. "The priesthood?"

Calvin smiled. "Not quite." He turned for the parking lot and the car he'd left there. He stopped and turned back to Marshall. "Oh, by the way, if I were you I'd give that one a new paint job and a new number. Might be some folks looking for her."

"Folks? What folks?"

But Calvin was gone.

Hugh was spread out on the couch in his office. Calvin could almost see the hangover surrounding him like a black cloud. Calvin shut the door quietly. Hugh cracked his eyes into slits, saw it was Cal and then shut them again.

"I'll be honest..."

"You didn't think you'd ever see me again," Calvin finished for him.

Hugh nodded slow to keep his brain from rattling.

"It's done. Have you heard anything?"

"A little. Cantrell's got no backup in place. They're already scattering to the wind. You broke their back, McGraw."

"I had help."

Hugh smiled. "Family. That's what Cantrell lacked. They can't break us because we got family."

Hugh's smile turned melancholy. His family was minus one more. When they'd lost Ennis in the war, the Stanleys figured they'd have only one martyred brother. Now they had two.

"Is that what you and I are, Hugh? Family?"

"We're tighter than most, McGraw. Tighter than most."

"In that case I need a favor."

Hugh rolled on his side and sat up with a series of groans fit for a man with two broken legs and a case of hemorrhoids. "You sure know how to take advantage of a guy."

"The girl Webb went to pick up—I need you to forget her."

Hugh chuckled a raspy, low sound. "I nearly had in all this mess."

"I'm serious, Hugh. She's free now. Deal?"

"Then we're square?"

It was Calvin's turn to smile. "Hugh, you and me are a lot of things but we'll always be nothing but crooked."

Hugh held out a hand and Calvin shook it.

Joni and Webb lay on his bed in the apartment over the garage. She was naked and droplets of sweat dotted her body. He hadn't gotten his pants all the way off. They were stuck around his ankles, caught on his boots he hadn't managed to kick off either once things got going.

"You just gonna lay there," Joni asked, "Or are you gonna get back up here?"

"Joni, honey, after the day I had I am tuckered out."

She rolled over, draped a hand across his chest and nestled her face into his neck.

"Hmm, Tucker. That's a good name for a boy, don't you think?"

About the Author

Eric Beetner is the author of more than a dozen novels, including *Rumrunners*, *The Devil Doesn't Want Me*, *When the Devil Comes to Call*, *Dig Two Graves*, *Run For The Money*, *The Year I Died Seven Times*, and *The Lawyer: Blood Moon*. He is co-author (with JB Kohl) of *One Too Many Blows To The Head*, *Borrowed Trouble* and *Over Their Heads*, and co-wrote *The Backlist* and *The Short List* with Frank Zafiro. He lives in Los Angeles.

CPSIA information can be obtained
at www.ICGtesting.com
Printed in the USA
FSOW01n1034071216
28275FS